Cyber Knot

Paige Etheridge

To my Grandfather, Dennis Mruz. A fellow Pisces who wouldn't trade his trip on Earth for the world.

2114

Prologue

The economy was in a slump. Population fell dramatically, and so have spirits. The government offers a generous stipend to working individuals to try the miracle drug, MX, meant to boost the economy. It worked. Productivity soared. The government was free of debt. This was the solution which would fix everything, the media cried. The population would soon recover. A few other countries tried MX as a result, while others avoided it feeling great consequence on the horizon.

They were right.

Users of MX lost their ability to focus on anything that wasn't work task oriented. Their relationships failed, they barely slept. Their spirits seem to be not repressed but erased entirely. Many worked themselves to death or became unable to shut themselves down until death did.

Yet new users continued to rise. The pay and government favoritism proved too tempting for many. Scientists worked to fix the drug as people continued to change and die; even if they stopped taking MX.

A subculture rose in rebellion against MX. They showed their distaste through replacing patches on their skin with clear prosthetics. Replacing whole organs came soon after they considered it a stronger form of protest. MX turned blood and organs blue. These were see-through parts to show your insides, proving MX never entered the body.

However, these modifications were illegal, since they often caused infection and death. Those found with the modifications were arrested and used to find others.

For the implants, there were drugs to prevent the rejection and infection of the body. However, these drugs were illegal and highly addictive. Other groups worked to take control of these substances. Drug abuse ran rampant. Morale hit an all-time low. Who wanted to raise children in the world now?

Nature maintained its power and control. Even during the periods humans thought otherwise.

Abandoned cities were conquered by vines and trees. People moved closer together in cities which maintained pockets of human life. A few roughed it out in the woods to get away from government jurisdiction. It's illegal, but with so much land now unoccupied and fewer people to patrol borders, not all of it could be put under surveillance at once. Some returned when they discovered how much harder it was to make it in the wilderness alone. While others never returned at all.

Most species aside from humans were protected under heavy environmental laws, but some felt these laws were no longer needed. However, with how bad things got before, or were thought to be, it was considered a bad political move to alter any environmental protection laws. New cities couldn't be built without huge political backlash. Nature was left to explode. While humanity was once again struggling to survive. Feeling lost and without purpose. They destroyed each other and themselves. The planets aligned for a new plague. But this time it wasn't tiny microbes, but drugs and technological induced suicide. Others were succumbing to any means necessary just to survive another day.

Like Keira.

Chapter One

I used to study missing person cases incessantly. Long before I should have known of such things. Back when I should have been enjoying electronic games and pretty creatures like butterflies. Instead I was using libraries and the internet for this hobby, among a few other ones such as studying the history of wars and carnivores.

I admired how these people were able to disappear, never to be seen again. I'm talking about the ones who weren't murdered or kidnapped. But people who clearly, or quite possibly, planned their escape. They freed themselves of the obligation of career, routine, and relationships. Even abandoning their country and government. Especially family, the big one culture still enforced but rarely fosters in a way which would get them functional. They were able to create a life of their own. A story not of the past, but of the future.

Had they left their past, unscathed? Probably not. It was still possible to be held back. The people you left behind now living inside your head. Still scorning. Still disappointed. Still ruling you.

Or you don't remember them much at all. Are you so naive that you make some deadly mistake of your own? Better off or worse? Perhaps it's all the same.

I hoped at least some of those people found freedom. Had a real life. Self-actualized or whatever.

Me? Well, I went from broken unwanted daughter, to sad lost girl, to criminal.

But either life spelt death for me anyway, I just didn't realize that before. Youth and inexperience can made you stupid. I'm not sure what was worse; being young enough to fall victim to someone's negligence or old enough to get yourself into a situation where someone was looking to kill you.

One day I found my backpack and decided which things I would take with me. It's amazing what becomes important when you know you're never returning to the same place again. A blue dream catcher the size of my hand. My only stuffed animal, a unicorn. The few clothes I liked most of which I found in a box labelled free. A flashlight. A notebook. A few cans of spray paint. A pack of M&Ms for the journey. There wasn't much food left in the house otherwise.

Everything else I left behind. The room I decorated in spray paint, but the art was so bad I was happy to leave it. It was just some stupid swirls, lines, and symbols anyway. Before I discovered my favorite colors. Hues of blue with touches of indigo. Blue is the rarest of the colors. You don't find it often in the natural world. Yet it's the vastness of the sky or the depth of the ocean. Both hold infinite dangers and possibilities. Blue had a special power no other hue contains.

I soon learned what you could really do with these colors. Not much else in the room. Just some scattered chaos. These were broken things, just like me. But hopefully I could be fixed. Unlike the things I was leaving behind, I might have a future.

After I left, little was done to find me.

I didn't see many missing posters for me, except on a few police bulletins. They were the only ones who seemed to care, and they were complete strangers. But the media didn't run my case. I know my family didn't care to find me. Perhaps they were relieved to have one less mouth to feed. To be rid of the kid who was a mistake. To only decide whether they were going to stick it out with each other or not. Or perhaps they were too drugged out on MX to even notice at all.

Police didn't spend too much time looking for runaways anymore. Even underage ones. So many kids vanished. So many people seemed to just walk off the Earth. Police were bombarded with so many things, it's hard for them to keep track. There are more people gone now than can be accounted for. More than those still going about their documented and electronically trailed everyday lives. There are so many theories why.

Our own evolutionary declined so only the strongest survived. The drug culture was bringing people to pleasure then pain, obscurity then death. Or simply people couldn't make time for child rearing between economic pressures and their own ambitions; working more or numbing themselves. Some were still trying to save humanity.

The population had at least stopped decreasing in the past five years. But it hadn't been going back to its old numbers. And there was no way it would be anytime soon it seemed.

Of course, there were the stupid conspiracy theories about people being eaten by the forest itself or something in it. Being drawn to it again as technology failed to fulfill them. Only to never be seen again. Was it the Wendigo? Bigfoot? Slenderman? Or people most likely dressing up pretending to be them, having been driven mad by the world around them?

I thought perhaps people went into the woods, so they never had to deal with other people again. Technology made people less likely to want to interact with each other. It turned many into loners. Perhaps living in the forest ensured they never had to deal with other people again.

I could account for only one of those who disappeared. I was among them, yet I still walked among those still tracked in the modern world.

***

I'm legally dead now. I was declared dead pretty quickly after my disappearance. There's even physical evidence of my death. Proving to the eyes of the law I'm long gone.

A bone fragment of my skull was found in an empty field. Reported anonymously through a call on a pay phone by someone who was probably not supposed to be there. At the time, it was believed I couldn't have possibly lived without it.

Even though my old gang is now linked to this technology, Police never reopened my case. What reason did they have to? They never made the connection I was part of the gang. Or knew it was Veronica from our gang, who made the call. Truthfully, few of those reproduced copy parts were used to make missing people seem dead anyway. Cops were busy with bigger things on their plate. Much of the country was drugged out as well as dying. It was a mess sorting it all.

***

At the time, I wondered why this nameless gang was willing to take in a thirteen-year-old. Later I learned just how I young I really was, even if I felt otherwise. My mind was ready to be molded, but I was old enough to be angry. The rage was fuel which was thought to be useful. They needed more bodies. Their continued loyalty to those clear prosthetics were costing lives. They realized they needed at least some of their members without the drug or implants, or their message would be snuffed out. Young people were the least likely to be touched by either.

But with me, it was mostly my unquenchable rage.

That's what attracted Conroy to me. He found me bashing old electronics with a bat as I was taking out my anger on the world. The parents who refused their role. The home which smelled worse with each passing day. My belly crying for substance. The school which refused me.

The library for kicking me out. I'd gathered these things from an abandoned building one by one, their weight nearly toppling me over. But I managed to heap them into a pile before getting to work. I was at it for a long time before I saw a blond man with aqua eyes watching me with a smile across his face. I later found out his ancestry was linked to Australia. Though he didn't speak with their accent, he left there when he was just a baby.

***

At the time, I thought he was an undercover cop, so I tried to flee. But he caught me before I could go anywhere. His speed caught me off guard. His strength pinned me to the brick wall. Fear coursed through my muscles and my anger was directed at him. My fighting proved useless, and after what felt like hours of struggle I finally was too tired to move any longer. He said he admired the fight still in me, and the life. Too many were already snuffed of their true nature at a young age. He carried my depleted body back to his hideaway to meet the others. Show me his world. Offer me a new life. Give me a banner under which my rage could be used for change. People to serve would also support me back. Even a promise my belly wouldn't always be empty.

Upon approval from the rest of his gang I was invited in.

Given a way out of my old life that was cut, clean, and final.

I could never go back after this. It was ensured I understood this. Death awaited me if I tried. I was all too willing to say yes, there was no deterrent for me at all.

I stayed with Conroy for a few days before I went back for my stuff.

Right before I went home for the last time, he taught me a game which involved playing catch with bats. This involved live bats, the kind that fly around. He told me those were the only bats I'd play with from now on. We threw tiny pebbles up to the night sky. The stars were blocked out by our stones, the bats caught them. They flew around us for a short while, before dropping them when they realize it wasn't something to eat. The trick was to follow those wings and catch the rock before it hit the ground. I was mostly successful. Which made Conroy seem proud. The pride made me all the more willing to go along with any plans he had for me.

    That was my last night as Keira.

***

Little was done to honor me by my family when the rest of the world thought I was dead.

    But I watched as the police pulled together a funeral for me. The same ones who had been on my case. They were solemn and respectful. Caring for a complete stranger. Perhaps they felt bad for someone so young with a shitty family and a terrible fate.

    There is a grave made of blue granite with my name and birthday on it. As well as an estimate day of death based on the piece of bone which was found with my DNA. Flying above it all is a carving of a butterfly. That fragment is buried somewhere below.

    It's located at Rainbow Valley, a cemetery for unloved and unknown children funded by the city. There's a rainbow of flowers, toys, and granite markers honoring the childhood they never got to have.

    I left flowers on my own grave once. On my birthday. Forget-Me-Nots were all I could find. They were growing wild close by at the time. I buried the roots into the Earth. I figured they'd be pulled out within a week. Yet they survived. Months would go by, my visits were usually infrequent, and I would still see them there, peering out as if to acknowledge my return. Over the years, they spread to other graves.

I saw someone else left flowers once. Blue roses. Those were always my favorites. Those couldn't grow naturally until a few decades ago. Scientist messing with plant genetics caused some to flood through the woods and urban areas. They were as hard to get to deroot as bamboo, so eventually attempts to get rid of them were halted.

Based off the smell on the stem, musky like sandalwood, I knew a young man left them. Though I don't remember knowing any in my old life who would have any thoughts for me. Or someone who remembered I loved blue roses. But that may be a coincidence all together; or a lucky guess. Or the flowers close at hand that day.

There was the one, but I doubted he even thought of me anymore.

I never saw my family there. I knew I didn't need to worry about running into them there. Which was why I visited my grave in the first place. It was one of the few places I could be alone and close to nature. The feeling I get there is hard to describe. The sense of finality brings me some grounding. My pain was going to end someday, just like the others here did. Here, trees only spoke through the wind. It was beautiful and peaceful. Death couldn't be so bad if this is what it had in store as a stark contrast to the pains and tragedies, as well as terrors, of life.

At night all the graves were luminescent. Lighting as the favorite colors of the deceased. Or a lucky guess of what it would be. Somehow mine was blue. Which made me happy. The glow made me glow inside.

Anytime of day, I could be free to think there without worries of dealing with anything. At least I had the illusion of that there.

However, I didn't spend too much time mourning my old life. I was focused on the new one. My new missions forced me to be.

And my new name.

Chapter Two

I was now Sky. Conroy let me take it when he asked about renaming me. I never found out what name he planned for me, he liked the idea behind mine too much. I wanted to be an embodiment of my favorite color. I wanted to be the sky, endless and free. Far above all the problems of humanity. Able to see the whole world from high up. Able to carry storms and sunshine. Moon and stars. Boundless and unstoppable.

I would be the sky in every way possible.

I kept my nails painted blue. The gang had a specialist who altered my genetics, so my hair would turn blue upon the addition of their special formula. Other girls used it, but they turned rotated their hair between hues of green, purple, white, or pink. I was the only one who wanted mine blue always. I stayed pale and skinny despite the promise of more food, but it just made my blue stand out more.

My eyes are already a rare combination of various blue hues. I swore no matter how safe, or tempting, I would never mess with my eyes. Those were the only real gift I'd ever been given by my parents.

I was given a second chance. I adorned myself on the outside hoping it would help me live up to my new identity. Yet I blew it all.

***

I didn't live up to my new name at all. I was embarrassed to even have it. I wanted to be Sky so badly. Fearless. Efficient in every task. Powerful. Unstoppable.

Instead I was considered a screw up at every turn. Except by Conroy. Or Aziel when he came along. I was at least able to stomach staying with their approval. I couldn't be that bad if the two men highest up still saw something in me.

2121

Chapter Three

Once I was old enough I became Conroy's lover. I'd foreseen this coming for a long time. In a way it was anticlimactic when it finally happened. I thought I should have been more excited. I knew I could never be fully a part of his world, but I thought we could share something to end the loneliness we both felt. Despite his cool demeanor, our age difference (he was close to thirty), his life on the wrong side of the law, I wanted to love him fully. He pulled me into his world and was taking me down with him. At least this was going to be an exciting ride.

My first time was in an alley. I hadn't quite finished a piece when Conroy appeared unexpectedly. His hands were on me swiftly. Mouth on mine, in sync. Back against the concrete. My shirt was already defying gravity. The rest of my clothes flew off, all that obscured me was his body in front of me and my artwork behind me. My world was spinning. My world was him. I was his.

He hadn't even asked me if the paint was dry. Modern paint could burn into your skin, become part of it. But it was more of a blob rather than a beautiful tattoo. Spray paint worked as tattoos for concrete and brick. Or he could have used my body to destroy what I just created.

The first time we made love was when I found out where his prosthetic was. It was the skin over his chest. He had some muscles replaced as well. I could see his heart beating fast for me. His human heart looked more like a bloated meat machine rather than something romantic. Still, I thought I saw his love for me underneath.

He told me I could touch it and I did. I felt a power to his bones but a vulnerability there over that beating organ, like a small hummingbird. Parts of him were surprisingly soft. It's as if I really was putting my hand inside his body, feeling what no one else could feel. Touching his very lifeforce.

The memory still took my breath away.

Looking back, I should have made sure the paint was dry.

He could have destroyed the piece.

Just like he destroyed the rest of me.

Once I had my surgery, things changed between us. He didn't kick me out, but he couldn't stand to look at me for long. Suddenly the favor he once held for me was gone. I was powerless to change it or understand why.

Chapter Four

Police were now looking for me. I'm not entirely sure why, but the few times I eavesdropped through the radio it only further proved my suspicions. Perhaps the worse was still out there to find me. At least the police tried to follow some justice. Some compassion. It would be sheer luck if the cops found me first or ended up being all I needed to worry about. It was likely my own gang was out to kill me. Though I couldn't know for sure.

I didn't have the option of going back to my old life either. I wasn't taken care of before, and I wouldn't be in the situation I was in now. There's good chance neither of my parents were even alive. Especially after all those years on MX and whatever else. Regardless, I was now a legal adult and had been for some time. I looked different, not like the unwanted kid they knew. They wouldn't believe it was me anyway. Or they would be too drugged out to do anything at all. Or they simply wouldn't want me. Perhaps they would even kill me themselves right then and there. Or call someone who would. Carbon copies of the dead were no longer common place, but it was still the law to eliminate them onsite.

Death was the main reason to avoid them. My remaining anger was another.

Not that I was unlikely to die with the path I was on. We all die. I wasn't sure why I was avoiding it. Survival instinct? Fear? A chance to keep painting?

I was more interested dying on my own terms. When I finally got the nerve to do myself in.

Or just keep existing. I wasn't entirely sure.

I resolved to make peace with my mortality. I was most likely going to be facing death soon.

And I was only twenty.

Chapter Five

Over the past few weeks, I'd been living under a bridge in my own little cupboard of concrete, vines, and graffiti. I was surrounded by my favorite color and glimpses of my version of the sky. Many of the worlds on the walls I created myself. With the cards I was dealt, this was likely to be the closest thing to having my own home I'd ever have. But it was still much prettier than my old childhood room. Even if it was damp and cold at night.

The eye candy would keep my mind off the discomfort of the surrounding elements. A maiden on a unicorn. Athena. Demeter. Waterfalls creating rainbows as they cascaded into pools filled with bottlenose dolphins and humpback whales.

These works were mine. They were of my creation. My choices. The best I'd been able to give to the world.

I wanted to be as close to them as long as possible.

Especially if these were my final days of freedom.

The finale of a screwed-up life.

Chapter Six

I tried to convince myself to paint. After all, I didn't know how much longer I had to live. These images were likely the only legacy I'd leave behind.

Graffiti was left to grow like weeds by citizen and government. This was after years of struggle and debate over it. People were doing it as a form of self-expression, as impulsive, emotional, and intimidating as a scream. The government simply couldn't keep up. At first government employees tried to wash it all away, only to find something new in the same spot the next day. The government even created light walls; black screen walls with tubes of light source secured to a hose. This was to give people a spot to release such impulses and create fake art in approved designated locations. Within a few years, they were used for advertising instead which were painted over with strong elements with crude remarks. Now this new paint couldn't be washed off those walls. Which hurt the companies of course. The light walls went out of commission quickly. They ended up buried under vines and graffiti like much of pervious society.

Police barley convicted anyone of the crime of painting outside anymore, hence why I knew they hadn't been chasing me for that. Even if it was a crime with a heavy penalty, I would have kept doing it. Painting was worth risking my life for over and over again.

The artwork spoke of the times, yet it was still beautiful. There was a type of hope to it too. Hence why it kept growing and expanding like the surrounding vegetation. It was constantly changing. A piece you love today could easily be gone tomorrow. Better take a picture or record it to memory. Occasionally if a piece was particularly good, it would be protected by others. Or if it was done in an abandoned area few frequented, it would likely remain untouched for years. But art could never last. Nothing could. Though my pieces seemed to last the longest.

Plants and graffiti now hugged buildings equally. Often blending together to tell their stories. Present their temporary art. Their contradictory images. Complementary colors. Flowers bursts open. Paint colors exploded. Vines reached into every crevice.

Nature and urban life both worked to expand to the furthest of its abilities. But no matter how advanced technology got everything returned to earth, in final destruction and death. But from there life began again. Plants grew out of the homes where the families died off long ago. A memorial was painted to honor a dead friend, which inspired art out of someone else. Flowers planted at a grave expanded to places the dead hadn't ventured in life but perhaps wanted to go. Paint finally gave another form of life a chance to grow. There was so much meaning, even in all its silence.

Which is why I'd become a graffiti artist myself.

The colors were bright and unapologetic. The canvas, the gritty backdrop of our true environment, our true world. No Photoshop here. Everything was left real and bold. Art imbedded amongst the grit of the real world and made its home there. Its existence could cause a moment of laughter, a moment of remembrance, anger, or sadness. Hope, above all else, we could still create a beautiful world. The best pieces inspired others to be better for themselves and the world. Not a lot of really motivated people anymore. Hence why the government put them on drugs. Art still did though. The government should have funded it for the sake of morale instead.

While painting, I was comfortable being as loud, rude, or beautiful as I wanted. I could attempt to balance my different sides or disregard those lines entirely. The masculine and feminine. My dirty street self and the refined artist longing to emerge from the inside. The beautiful world I longed for, which I could only create on a two-dimension format. This I'd leave on a wall. Showing others such a personal part of me without them ever meeting them. Perhaps this outlet made it easier to hide. It was simply allowing me to leave the mark of my existence in a beautiful way, despite my chaotic and hard life. The choices I made with my paints were the only ones I could be proud of on a regular basis. Even the risky ones.

For my work nature was a test. I loved to tag places right before a major storm or earthquake. If the piece survived, it was nature's way of saying it was worthy of survival. Worthy of being art. I'd return after to see what had been cracked, what was torn apart. What was made dirty or cleaned through the storm? What was left entirely intact? A few times a piece was improved by the additional imperfections. A few times to my relief, a piece was completely shattered, giving me a chance to start anew. When a piece I loved was destroyed I took it as a sign to do better. When one was saved it was a sign for at least for now, what I created was enough.

There was the thrill in feeling the earth trembling beneath my feet. The mist of an oncoming storm, threatening to wash away the paint before it had time to dry. Booming skies rocking my very core. It pushed me along. Kept me from overthinking. My life could depend on it. It was the only thing I was willing to risk my life for, to die for. I wouldn't do that for my gang, but I'd do it for my art.

Few people covered my tags. Even business owners seem to keep my work. Even when I broke in to do it. I think a few have even gotten improved business over it. I'd check in after.

I drew hearts and beautiful women. Strong men. Forests and Oceans combined with art. Things which I knew existed, but often felt so far from me. Concepts and realities which I couldn't possess. Things I couldn't be.

***

Yet I just couldn't get myself to paint then. The stress of survival was too much. The idea of even painting made my body quake. I had to face perhaps it was no longer going to be possible for me. The tags I made were all I was going to ever create. Eventually they would be washed out of existence, just like me.

Chapter Seven

I woke up. As my hand ran over my face I felt my hair. Grungy. But not cool grungy. This was homeless grossness. That's never sexy. Even if I did feel like touching a pizza.

It's not like I could go to a public bath house as much as I wanted to. The thought of a mud bath temporarily relaxed my muscles, before despair kicked to remind me it wouldn't be happening now or likely ever again. Though there were ways I could bath which involved less risk, even if there was still consequence upon getting caught.

I started making my way to the river.

From what I remembered, cops didn't patrol the border by the river around this time. They mostly did at night. Or times when people were most likely to be depressed about the city life, like a Monday. It was assumed people came here to end their lives rather than start anew in the wilderness.

I slipped under a hole in the concrete fence. It didn't matter that I was getting covered in all dirt as I slid over the earth. A cool wash of water was waiting for me. I reached the river at the edge of the forest. It was beautiful but haunting. I've heard a lot of stories about people trying to rough it in the woods and not making it. Or search parties looking for people only to find dead bodies in the woods. Some from suicide. Some from being ripped apart by wild animals. Or maybe something worse.

I undressed. I shivered as I looked at the wood and then the water. I dipped into the river.

The coldness shocked me at first, but then numbs the pain over my whole body. I felt a swirl over the spot where the surgery left its mark.

Then I let myself go.

The currents pressed into me and pulled to keep me afloat. I was flying while remaining on the earth. Skydiving in place. In a world all my own. I never wanted it to end.

There had been a trend a few years back in which a bunch of people pushed lawmakers to allow humans to modify themselves, so they could become cyborg mermaids. I wasn't sure what the results were. I hadn't seen any humans with fish tails; real or robotic.

I let my mind flow like the current around me. Let my head stay in the dream for a while.

***

I emerged from the water and walked to the edge of the forest to the south. This would be a peaceful place to die for sure. But I didn't want to ruin such a beautiful place with my corpse. I watched the woods for hours. Foxes and hawks made themselves known. I heard frogs and the cry of eagles.

Still soaking it in, I returned to the water. I wondered what it would be like to rough it in the woods. Would I be safe in the wilderness? Free? Perhaps if I could learn to feed myself out there, found shelter, and brought some weapons. Made friends with the creatures. I could make a real life out there. Find real peace and happiness. I laughed at the thought. My first laugh in a while.

Crunch.

I'd let my guard down for far too long. The pain in my surgical spot flared until I saw white. It took me a moment to process what was coming. But the radio gave it away.

Cops!

I slipped as I jumped back into my pants, then my socks. My shoes needed more careful tending than I liked. My shirt only slipped back on as I began to run with my backpack in hand.

The cops were tracking me. Their voices almost echoed within me as they got closer.

I threw my underwear into the woods. I sent a scent decoy, the last in my pocket, after it into the woods so the dogs would track elsewhere. It was one of many tricks my gang members used to get away from danger. I pressed the vile too hard, so it cracked too soon, cutting my fingers in the process. The blood trail was going to make me easier to track once the dogs figured out the trail was a fake.

As I ran, my hearing soon proved they hadn't gone for my underwear or even the decoy. They still were trailing me. Dogs are far from stupid animals. They figured out to ignore those decoy smells long before the cops did. Or they found my blood first. It was useless. I should have known better.

But I still had enough time to get away. Slipping right under the same spot in the wall I came in from. I scraped my back against concrete. A jolt of pain only temporarily distracted me from my plight. Then I was running again.

I experienced another pain which distracted me from my injuries. I hated running. I did it way too often. A life of crime leads to a life of running; otherwise death or a cage awaited. As much as it hurt, no matter how much painful it was, no matter how much I wanted to stop and cry, I had to keep going.

***

It would be too risky to go back to my main base tonight. I needed to stay elsewhere.

I proceeded to head north to an old building. This was a place I'd scouted a few months ago in the event of situation just like this. There were others I could have gone to, but it was as if something in this building was calling out to me. I went with the hunch.

Just like many others, this building was turning green as nature took back what was always hers. There weren't enough people and businesses to occupy these old buildings. Eventually the elements would eat away at these constructs entirely. But for now, in this area, they remained at least somewhat hospitable. These were the ghosts of a shrunken down population, being slowly consumed by the greenery. The Earth was taking back its rightful place in the modern world.

There was still a helicopter pad on top of the roof. It was covered in graffiti and vines. Only a miracle would get it to fly again. A huge painting covered the whole building which poked out from under the green. A T-Rex jumped at helicopter from beneath. Raptors circling its feet. A tribute to the past. Or our own technological dinosaurs.

A tiny push and the doors at the entrance opened for me.

Chapter Eight

The first few flights of stairs were overcome with moss and ferns. Civilization looked like it was back in control by floor six. This would be the floor I would find settlement for the night. The carpet still smelled of soap. There must have been a ton of self-cleaning spray used here before they abandoned this place. It clearly hadn't evaporated yet. Offices turned to that cleaner like hospitals turned to bleach. It took years for the smell to go away.

It also made it hard for dogs to track my smell.

The office chairs and cubicles looked as if people could be coming in for another day of boredom and misery, or if they were on the drug, another day of being an efficient soulless robot. If it wasn't for the layer of dust icing the desks. The self-cleaner was still efficient only on the floor it seemed. I was surprised. This area would be prime for robbers and scavengers and vandals. Why had no one touched this spot yet?

I should have been nervous. But again, a cop would have found me by now if this spot was being scouted or if the carpet cleaner failed to mask me. Maybe everyone assumed this spot had been pillaged already. A lot of these buildings looked the same. Their individuality was the growth and art that covered them which changed over time.

I found a sealed off room. The door still had a lock which wasn't going to give easy without a key or a fight. Working with two tiny metal prongs from my pack, I won and pried it open, forcing the ghost out of the old lock at last. Perhaps it was relieved.

A desk and black chair faced me as I entered the room, prompting me to close the door behind me. A Zen garden with tiny basalt stone and a mahogany colored rake topped the desk. It was barren aside from that. There were no photos of any family or anyone else. Not even a desk lamp. Bookshelves line both sides in the back, still full of books. Who would have left all of those behind? No icing of dust but I couldn't smell the cleaner in here.

In front of the bookshelf is a brown couch with a touch of shine. Couldn't tell if this was fake leather or that cell reproduction one. I laid my bag out at the foot of towards the self. If I needed to make a quick getaway in the middle of my slumber I could avoiding tripping over it but be close enough to grab it. I pulled out the antiseptics and bandages to treat my injuries. Once I did that, I assessed everything else.

The ceiling was an eggshell white. To the left of the bookshelf was a fully filled vending machine. I couldn't believe my luck in finding one in such pristine condition. I broke into this one without too much guilt, despite a nagging moment recognizing I was creating destruction in this still pristine room.

I spied at the treasures which were now free of the glass casing. Plenty of junk food. My eyes lit up. At least tonight, I would be getting a decent meal. Dessert for the first time this year. The desk was empty except for a water heater inside the bottom drawer. A plug next to the coach made its red light go on. I'd also would be getting a warm meal tonight.

I had three packages of ramen, a giant can of Arizona Iced Tea, two package of S'mores Pop Tarts, two packs of Fig Newtons, and a Snickers bar. That's one thing which hadn't changed over the years; the things lurking in vending machines. A buffet of high calorie food. Which I needed now. I ate with reckless abandon.

I felt happily full and grossly sick at the same time. All that food at once messed with my stomach. I was so used to being hungry, being full was sometimes more painful. But once it subsided, happy fullness made me content for the moment.

Any extra food, I stuffed into my pack. Every last pack of Pop Tarts, Ramen, and candy bars were shoved into the mouth of my pack which expanded willingly for this purpose. I strove to travel light, even leaving most of my paints behind with the exception of some blue I couldn't part with, but I needed to ensure this food stayed with me. I never knew when my next meal was coming. For now, I at least had something to lift my spirits.

It would be tempting to stay here long term, it was a lovely shelter from the elements to store my wares and hide myself from the world. I was imaging how I could repaint these walls, turning them into a forest which transitioned to a beach and then an ocean. Perhaps there were more vending machines still intact on other floors. Yet I knew in my gut eventually someone would find me here, either cop or criminal. Neither would let me stay. I couldn't retain territory over a whole building. I wasn't strong enough.

I plopped onto the coach. My eyes rose to the ceiling, I didn't notice my hand had wandered to where my implant was, until the pain alerted me. This was a recent habit of mine which only started a few months ago, when the chip was placed inside me. I kept my hand there. It made the blue of my nail polish stand out more. Giving them a glow.

I'm wondering what it's doing there inside my body. This alien part of me. My own internal mystery. Something a part of me as much as my heart and brain but didn't belong there. I never consented to it being there either.

Chapter Nine

I'd returned from a job Conroy tasked me to do. I finished early and was ready to report. It seemed so important to me at the time but looking back I couldn't remember what it had been about anymore.

I entered our interrogation room where Conroy told me to meet him. I didn't see him and only felt him when grabbed me from behind. I didn't dare scream as he pinned me to the wall. I suspected he was placing me for a spontaneous sex session. The mood would hit him suddenly and especially if no one was around, he saw no qualms pulling me into a secluded corner and having his way with me. Sometimes I even found it a bit romantic. But this time he was holding me so tight against the wall it hurt.

Before I had the chance to prepare myself, I saw Aziel behind us. His silver eyes shown out and drew my attention to him. He held a blank look on his face. There was nothing for me to read there.

Embarrassed, I tried to tell Conroy not proceed. I certainly didn't want anyone watching such a private act. But before I had a chance, Aziel shot a needle into my arm. I cried out from shock and pain as my eyes blurred while I fell to the floor.

"Are you sure about this?" I heard Conroy say.

"She's more ready than you know." Aziel replied.

"It's her favorite color at least."

My mind fell into darkness.

***

When I woke up, I found myself on a cold metal table surrounded by whiteness. I was in our gang's medical facility, as I realized upon closer look. My mind swirled.

A throbbing pain alerted me to a change in my body. Had I'd been given prosthetic skin against my will? Had my organs been replaced? I would likely die soon if that was the case.

With my left hand I found the stitched spot underneath my navel which certainly wasn't there before. It felt like there was a rock underneath. Nothing had been taken out, no body part changed. Something was put inside me instead.

I was too drugged out to scream.

***

Despite my lifestyle, I'd managed to keep my skin completely smooth, pristine, scar free. This was no longer the case and I resented it. Alone in the aftermath of this mysterious surgery, lucid thoughts poked through like flashlights within the cloudy haze, I heard the door opening. Aziel entered the room. The look on his face was soft, kind even. My confusion compounded further.

"How are you feeling?" His voice tingled my spine. I jolted in response, hoping he didn't notice. That wasn't something I wanted to admit to him.

"I'm not sure." Why lie? I didn't have to hide for the answer at least.

He pulled up a chair to sit next to me, flipping it so the back was facing me, his arms folded over it. Even though it hurt, I sat up on the metal table. He protested subtly with a breath for a moment, but even with my wincing I still sat up too fast for him to get any words out. He relaxed once I was repositioned. My eyes were now aligned with his.

"What's going on?" My voice faded with each letter. I sounded as tired as I felt.

Aziel divulges the information to me slowly but carefully.

"You've had a chip implanted into your body. You proved to be the best candidate out of anyone else. You're the only one who could handle such an undertaking. It's an honor that you now have this...."

It's hard for me to process anything he's saying. It's as if I couldn't hear him. His words came in and out. But slowly the truth sunk in of what happened to me. I'd been chosen, based on tests I'd never even knew were occurring, for a special experiment dealing with the latest advances in cybernetic technology. All of which I knew nothing about, due to its top-secret nature. A plan I was a part of even if I didn't know or consent to the role I played. I was too disoriented to be afraid at the time. Or angry.

"You're ok." Aziel said as he put his hand to my shoulder. His eyes were still warm.

I noticed there was this strange humming between us. As if there was an electric current running from his body into mine.

"This is going to change your life for the better."

I wouldn't believe him even if I wanted to. I promised myself that.

***

A robo-nurse entered and prepared to test my vitals. Aziel left the room. I barely noticed the robo-nurse ejecting it's testing equipment, didn't even bother to look at the tests being run. My mind was on the humming from Aziel which dissipated as he grew further away. I felt as if I knew his exact route. Which I told myself was impossible. Then it stopped.

Chapter Ten

The first few days were the hardest.

I threw up all my meals. I couldn't even keep down applesauce. There was no sleep. Night and Day blended into each other so quickly, years could have gone by with how fast I felt it happening. I was in constant pain. I shook uncontrollably. I screamed and cried, but still felt no relief.

Test after test from the robo-nurses proved my body was fine. I was even responding better than expected to the chip. It was determined I was just having an intense psychological reaction to the surgery. I was moved into a room with a bed and window meant to make me more comfortable. I wanted to tell them it was a normal reaction to being violated. Panicked at having something inside me I didn't want or understand. But robots didn't care. No one else likely would either.

Conroy never visited. Neither did anyone else from the gang.

Aziel was the only one. He came to see me daily, sometimes more. Every time he was close I felt the humming again, informing me he was coming this way. I didn't ask him about it. I figured I was just going insane. If it was suspected I might have gone crazy, I could be trapped here or worse for a long time. He didn't understand the horror of what happened to me. He was one of the reasons I was at this point. How could I expect him to understand the hum? Despite its growing more intense each time, I pretended it wasn't happening.

He seemed to be analyzing me hard each time. Waiting for me to speak or say something. He'd ask me questions which I wouldn't respond to or my brain was so hazy I just didn't hear them. Was he just seeing how this experiment was going to go? I didn't know. The intensity of his gaze and attention made me feel vulnerable to him. Entirely naked. He seemed to see my whole world and mind. As if he knew what I was really feeling.

I just told myself to ignore what my intuition already knew. He knew exactly what was happening to me. Yet, he did nothing to ease my suffering.

***

The last time he came, new sensations arose in me.

It was as if I could see imagines from his past projected from his mind. A surgery he had endured as a child. Technology imbedded in him against his will. I told myself it was a gnarly hallucination. Aziel seemed angry when I had this thought. He was directly responding to my thoughts now. Once he sensed my fear, he calmed back down. Other sensations were apparent to me now as he sat there with me. There was no longer the hum. But a full current between us.

I was feeling sympathy. Affection. Longing.

Even arousal.

He reached over to touch me where the chip was. His hand sent a tingling sensation into the chip and through the rest of my body as he inched closer and closer. I pulled away.

"You feel it now too, don't you?"

I said nothing in turn.

"I'll take care of you, Sky. You're mine to protect now."

He sent the message directly to my mind. I remained blank in turn.

He left. I wasn't sure what he was feeling then. He probably didn't either.

This needed to end.

***

That night I decided the chip was coming out whether I lived or died in the process. I'd taken a knife I'd retrieved from one of the robo-nurses who malfunctioned and left their equipment exposed all at once. I'd managed to snag it before it was sent to be fixed.

I undid the stitching with the knife. It didn't hurt until my skin was entirely splayed opened. I dug my fingers inside my own bloody mess, biting my lip to keep from screaming. I found the chip with my fingers. But as I went to pull it out, it wouldn't emerge. A few tugs proved it wasn't because of my grip. Fingering the chip revealed tendrils were emerging from it and rooting itself into my body.

Before I could begin cutting away at these, Aziel burst into the room. Within moments he'd slapped the knife out of my hand, pinned me down, and tied me to the bed. He was already cleaning the wound when the robo-nurses entered. He was shouting at them words I didn't care to understand.

How had he known what I'd been up to? I thought he could only read me from close by. I wanted to ask him. Right then and there. But this wasn't what came out of my mouth.

"Why did you do this to me?" Tears blurred my vision.

He didn't answer.

His hand covered in my blood, stroked the side of my face and sent a current right into my brain. He pushed his forehead against mine and the current increased in intensity. He'd managed to stop me from crying and calm me. He then lulled me to sleep.

***

I awoke to find the stitching had been re-done with a metal like substance. It couldn't be cut except by special tools. I was left powerless to alter what had been done. I was left like that for days until the chip fully settled. At that point, I wouldn't be able to remove it. It's what Aziel told me.

I gave up on removing it. Stopped resisting this piece of technology which was now part of me and decided to face my fate.

The day finally came when Aziel removed the stitching himself. Only a small white line of a scar remained. It looked as if I'd only been touched by snow.

"You wouldn't have any scarring if you hadn't hurt yourself like that." His finger traced me there.

"I didn't opt to have a chip put there."

"No. But in time, you'll understand."

He continued to stroke me there. My body didn't even try to resist him. It was as if my cells were drinking him in, eager for more with every swallow. I tried to ignore the charging sensation I felt. Nothing could be trusted. Even my own feelings. He was messing with my internal circuits somehow. What mattered anymore?

I looked at the window outside. Wondering when I'd be able to go paint again.

Chapter Eleven

Things subsided slowly. I started having full meals of applesauce without throwing up. Water went down easily. I upgraded back to sandwiches and lasagna. Hospital food didn't taste so bad when you hadn't tasted real food in weeks.

I was released from my prison and allowed into the world once more. There were no jobs from my gang. What I'd endured, and continued to endure, was enough of a job for them for now. I didn't feel like seeing or talking to them anyway.

The free time I had I filled just fine.

I bought some new colors. Silvers and Golds. Loud neon's for each color of the rainbow. I found a wall and painted Hera washing herself to be freed. Away from Zeus and all he'd done. The water splashing around her face. The joy of being in the water. Feeling it all around her. Freedom in her solitude and healing.

I was proud of what I created.

All I wanted to do was paint. Besides eating and sleeping, that's all I did for months. On walls I told the stories of the Goddesses. Artemis. Athena. Demeter.

All my mind allowed for was shapes and colors.

I avoided Aziel to the best of my abilities. He stayed away. But I often felt him. Even when he wasn't close by.

***

When I wasn't painting, the currents from the chip working through my body became more apparent. I'd feel a calm sea inside me, then a stormy ocean of electricity. The roots worked deeper into me for the first month, and then settled where they were. But those currents grew more and more intense. I felt like a volcano on the verge of eruption, closer to blowing each day. After a few months, even painting wasn't enough to keep my mind off them anymore.

I worked up the nerve to confront Aziel about all of this. I knew I could never fully corner a guy like him into submission. But perhaps he would at least tell me something. I needed relief. I needed answers.

I used the chip to trail him. He wasn't too far.

Aziel was grinning as I approached him. Before I had a chance to say anything he caught my waist with his hands.

Somehow, he wasn't hurting me, even though he was touching my most sensitive part where the chip remained buried. I felt the tingle off from him again. I found myself leaning into him as he felt for the chip. My head relaxed next to his.

I caught my lips brushing against his.

I pulled away as I realized what I was doing. I looked down at our feet.

"Sky." I felt him moving his face to meet mine again.

I pushed him away and ran. Even though it hurt. Even though I didn't want to. Something told me if I got far away enough, got enough distance between us, he wouldn't be able to find me for a while. I just kept going north. I let the colors and sounds blur around me as the pain of running took over.

I went straight for a painting I hadn't visited in years. It was one of my first. I didn't have too many tags in this area since this wasn't a part of the city I frequented. Finally taking time to breath, my head rested against Eireen, who was surrounded by orcas.

I could still feel the charge where Aziel's hand ran over the chip. I wanted to run right back to him. Finished what I started. Explicit thoughts of him coursed through my mind. Thoughts of having him inside of me, having all of me, having all of him.

I wanted him, and I was utterly terrified.

I slept in a concrete cubby right across the Eireen and her ocean. Most of the painting was still the same. But some of the orcas now have cybernetic parts. Lazer eyes, robotic tails, titanium plates. All of their eyes watching me was a comfort regardless.

After what happened with Conroy, he dropped me after the surgery without a word. Feelings like these would be better to run from. There was nothing good in it for me in the long run. Especially since things were just so much more complicated with Aziel.

I still didn't have any answers.

No matter what happened, my feelings stayed just as strong for him. My mind was continuously drawn back to him again and again.

As well as what he had done to me.

Chapter Twelve

At night, the pain of the chip returns. My mind would be forced back to the questions I avoided. What did this thing do? How was it changing me? How responsible was I for it? What did Aziel know that he hadn't yet told me? What was this mystery I was mothering?

But this night, I pushed those thoughts away. I wanted to simply enjoy the pleasure of sinking into a comfortable couch. Allowing myself to be lazy. Feel safe. This was a luxury I rarely was given the opportunity to indulge in. Something so many exploited. I'd never even gotten the chance to be a couch potato. Even though that was supposed to be a contagious curse upon our modern world.

I could hear the city outside. People screamed in anger. Shouts turned to fights. Crashing glass. Police arrived with their electric new cars with the metallic sound that also seemed to follow them. I only tensed for a moment as I realized they're not looking for me and I should be relieved they were occupied with other things. A chivalric obligation to save a damsel in distress. A quieter night ensued once the men were locked in handcuffs and the woman was sent off to safety far away. The sounds had shifted to outdated car horns, the hum of vehicles, the clatter of deliveries being made.

Occasionally some nature sounds peaked their way through since I was so close to the woods. I recognized the swish of movements and the nightly cries. I let all that soothe me and be my lullaby.

***

I dreamt I was part of a tribe of Native Americans. I knew their language. Knew their names for all the trees and rivers. The freshest food passed between my lips. I had a job creating new weapons. I even had time to paint on wood and clay. The landscape inspired me. I felt useful and happy.

But a storm was brewing. Not from the sky above but from something inside me. Something which lit me up on the inside. Lightening burst out of me. I feared it would kill my tribe, so I ran away. They called my name. I ran deeper and deeper into the woods. I didn't know how this power was coming from me and I didn't know how to control it. I stopped when my breathing became too hard to keep going. I was then consumed by light. White light which then shifted into yellow and then...

Chapter Thirteen

Orange flames glared at me from the other side of the open door.

After remembering I closed the door, I scanned around to assess the situation I was in.

Fire hadn't entered the room yet, but the other side was full of flames. Smoke was infiltrating the room I was in. I wouldn't last here for long.

I grabbed my stuff and booked it.

As I exited the office I saw the rest of the building was a bright clementine glow. The heat cut into me like the chill of a cold day. The bursts of fire made it hard to breathe.

At least I was rescuing all of that sugar and chocolate. Hopefully, there weren't vending machines still full of goodies about to be eaten by flames.

The artificial indoor rain spouted from the ceiling sprinklers. I sighed in relief. Sure, I'd still need to leave, or the police could try to pin me for arson I didn't commit, but I could perhaps return. The tension in my body calmed and my heart slowed down. That was until I noticed the spray wasn't weakening the fire. The blaze was turning green and intensifying. It clearly wasn't water coming from the ceiling. The whole system had been rigged.

I didn't need to know how it happened or why. I just needed to get out.

I made it to the stairs and ran down several flights. Despite the sound of the fire, I was alerted to a familiar musky sandalwood like smell. I told myself I didn't have time for this as I ran down the hall on the third floor. The smell led me to a room. By the back wall was the kind of bag you'd see at a morgue. The zipper was tied shut so I cut the bag open with a knife from my pocket. I was making sure wasn't a puppy or something. Or possible supplies I could rescue for my own use.

Below me was an unconscious man who was tied up and gagged. His dark hair was hidden in the shadows of the fire. I untied him. I slapped him, so he'd wake up. It didn't work. I could feel he was alive. I shook him until his eyes opened.

"We got to go," I said as I brought him to his feet.

At first, he looked at me in a daze. I assumed it's because he woke up in a strange place surrounded by fire. I probably looked similar upon waking as well. Perhaps he was thinking it could all be a dream just as I did.

When I moved my hand off him my eyes were drawn to a mark.

Then I noticed it was a tattoo.

He was one of the Jackals.

Chapter Fourteen

When I was young I'd imagine their symbol to be a Celtic knot of a fire dog. Teeth dripping with blood, skin scorched from flames, hell in his eyes. I'd have nightmares about it a few times. Being chased by such a demon beast. Losing the fight for my life. Consumed alive in his burning stomach.

At the time I thought symbols were supposed to be complicated. But emblems were simple designs quick to send a message, until my elaborate paintings. I learned that later. How quickly people saw a simple image which conveyed such a strong reaction so quickly. Such terror within an instant of recognition.

I'd been hearing about this organization long before I ran away. There were stories about them dating far back enough that they were considered legends. Individually they survived harsh terrain and weather all over the world. Swam through floods. Navigated through blizzards. Knew dozens of languages. Could deal without water, food, and air longer than any other human who ever lived.

Together they were an unimaginable terror. Overthrew entire governments. Fought tanks and tigers with their bare hands. Had the power to bomb entire planets to dust. Their powers were unmatched. Individuals and nations feared them equally. Even their allies walked a fine line to ensure relations remained on good terms. It could turn deadly otherwise.

These tales were taken as fact. No one dared to question them. History proved over and over again that those who stood against them, got washed away in blood.

My gang introduced me to their real symbol early in my training. A Jackal emerging from the flames. Brown fur accented with a black stripe along its back. Ready to pounce on the next prey. Exposed because it didn't matter. They were the powerful animals here.

I did my own research as well.

Black Back Jackals were the most aggressive of the Jackals. Which is what this army choose this as their symbol. Their long standing position along the evolutionary path. Their efficiency as hunters. Their brutality in killing.

Jackals were survivors of both the ancient and modern world. Of wilderness and concrete jungles. Despite changing terrains and times, they always made it through. Even when the world was a wild jungle. Even when it was being fully industrialized. Even as it was returning to its wild nature. Perhaps we could have learned something from them.

Instead, everyone in our gang were under strict order to kill any Jackals onsite. No hesitation. No mercy. That's how they dealt with us and that's how we were supposed to be right back. Ideally a brutal death was told to be inflicted, and we were promised great reward. Even though fighting them was useless. They'd killed off so many of our members. We never stood a chance against them. I figured other methods of dealing with them would be better. Perhaps find the reason they wanted to kill us, work it out, and team up instead. I knew better than to argue with Conroy. His way was the only way.

When one was coming for you, there was nothing you could do. You were the one who was dead meat.

Ironic considering the situation we were in. This Jackal would have been the dead one here if I hadn't released this wild dog.

Wait, why had I done that?

I released a Jackal on myself. And I didn't even have a head start.

Chapter Fifteen

The Jackal grabbed my hand. Before I could process what's happening, we're running down the last flights stairs. For now he wasn't looking to kill me. Perhaps he thought I was a normal civilian. These Jackals were supposed to be somewhat heroic too. They generally stayed away from the general public but would aid them in grave circumstances. Conroy hadn't told me that, my research had. I just had to keep my own marks hidden and I could slip away once we made it outside. He never had to find out anything else about me.

As we exited I noticed the flames were turning blue. That is a horrible sign. Someone set up the right chemicals to get this whole building to blow up. Someone who was an expert at creating chemical fires; higher class of criminal than regular arsonist. This fire could burn through fire proof materials with no problem. Any trace of what this place had once been, would be gone before the fire department could attempt any rescue.

I think of all the food which would have melted. It would have been a tragedy. I patted my pack as we made it outside just to ensure my treasure trove were all still there.

We ran to a hill with an eagle's eye view of the building. We watched in silence in the distance as the chaos ensues. It was tragic how my temporary haven was so quick to turn into a fiery inferno death trap. That was just my luck in life though. Anything beautiful was only temporary, but the pain was forever.

My need for rest and air brought my knees to the earth. The man had released me. My eyes were now on the grass attempting to slow down my thoughts. I only caught a few breaths before the Jackal pulled me to my feet to face him. I did know those eyes. It was impossible for anyone to have the same swirl of Indigo. He ripped off the sleeve of my shirt. The mark from my gang was clearly illuminated from the fire despite the deep night. The diamond dripping in blood and my number inside, 82, etched into my skin.

I felt the hollow silence of the next few moments. Waited for what he'd do next. He pulled a gun to my head. Angry eyes were inside of mine. We were a world of emotional blue all our own. My heart ached for his pain there. I didn't feel this was a typical reaction to one's about to be executioner.

I'd been an idiot to help this guy. Perhaps this was a call Conroy was right about all along.

This was it. Despite the feel of the barrel against my temple, my life wasn't flashing before my eyes. No profound thoughts or good last words were coming to mind.

The Jackal looked at me for a long moment. I waited for him to shoot or say something. Part of me debated telling him to hurry up and just do it. End my misery. At least I'd finally be free. My desire to cling to life despite its challenges was a prison and torture enough. What rewards was in sight except being able to say I made it through yet another day? It was pointless.

I pushed my head into the gun and kept our eyes locked.

At least I had a warm place to sleep and a full belly before this.

But he retracted his gun. Eyes still on mine he returned the gun to a hidden pocket in his long black jacket before beginning to tie my hands together. He gagged my mouth and returned me to the earth to finish with binding my legs.

I heard sirens. Perhaps he heard them before me and knew killing me here would have been too risky. Though it was doubtful a Jackal would have to fear normal emergency responders of any kind. Still it would make things easier if he finished me off elsewhere.

Unless I found a way out.

Chapter Sixteen

He threw my pack over his left shoulder and me over his right. He started to run. Faster than I could imagine any man could considering the weight of me and all the junk food. I would haunt him not for killing me, but for eating any of that food after he did so. I caught a whiff of his curly black hair. I knew the smell, but I still couldn't figure out what drew me to him and got me into this mess.

My blonde hair meshed with his dark. That was also a familiar sight.

This wouldn't help me right now.

I abandoned the inquiry and returned my mind to survival. I could still get myself out of this. My body was heating where the tape was, making it easier for me to slip out. I barely worked at my binding, so he wouldn't notice. Was this the chip's doing or an act of God? I wouldn't question it right then.

My hands and mouth were now free.

I used his back to give myself the momentum to flip myself over him, before retrieving my knife and cutting my legs free. As he turned around I was already running ahead of him. While I hated to run, I was always much faster than most humans. I booked it for the labyrinth of alleys which ran through the abandoned part of the city. I knew this maze better than anyone. Their walls were my canvas. After a few minutes without looking back, I finally realized with a quick glance he'd lost me.

I sighed in relief as a slugged my body against a brick wall with a particularly angry purple faerie I'd created was cut short. Then I remembered the man still had my pack.

Except for the knife still in my hand, all my supplies were gone.

***

Why had I helped that guy anyway? It wasn't like me to do something like that. Perhaps shooting me would have been too much of a favor.

I headed back to my main tunnel home. I'd stash some back up supplies there. No food, but I'd had some tools that at least could help me figure everything else out. I was running again to reach my concrete cubby. I could feel myself drifting to sleep in my spot already. I was too tired to be devastated not having the coach anymore or the pile of junk food. I was only a few hundred yards away when I saw lights flooding the area. It was also flooded with cops.

I blended back into the shadows and headed back up to my spot to the south.

When I reached my other backup spot, it was flooded with cops as well. I ran back to the labyrinth of alleys deeper in the city.

Daybreak was stinging my eyes. I was tired with nowhere else to go. I walked into an alleyway, sat next to a trash bin, and sobbed.

***

I was all alone with no supplies. The police were checking each of my bases. I was outmatched. I would be found soon, for whatever reason they wanted me. There's only so long I'm going to be to keep running until I collapsed. Before I was dragged to a cage or death. There was no way I'm going to last any longer.

Aziel popped into my mind.

"Call Aziel." Was it my mind saying it or the chip?

I told myself I couldn't. He wasn't what I needed. He'd only make things worse.

Pain tore through my mind and I landed on the concrete below. I could barely breathe.

"Call Aziel. Call Aziel. Call Aziel." My mind echoed this over and over. I couldn't hear any other thought in my mind. It was taken over by static.

Soon the thoughts became "Call me," in Aziel's own voice.

I shouldn't do it. That's what I told myself. But I just wanted the pain to stop.

To the south I found a payphone and called the magic three number.

Chapter Seventeen

Rubbing my forefinger against the phone wire was comforting, as if I could coax the call. Make this all easier. Coax him to pick up.

Aziel answered. The static quieted and I sighed as the rest of the pain washed away. I could tell by his exhale he felt something lifting as well. He breathed in such a way I heard some of the deepness of his voice. He was just short of saying something. He did it powerfully and quickly. I felt a tingle in a spine. I still heard what he'd planned, just in my mind.

I shook my head. This was a bad idea. I wasn't going to hang up though. I didn't have any other options. I allowed Aziel to be a comfort. Felt myself succumbing to his pull.

I got to the point fast, "The police are looking for me."

He left no chance for pause. I felt his anger before he uttered the first syllable.

"Could you explain why I haven't been able to find you in the past few weeks?" He said, "Or why you haven't contacted me? I thought you were dead! Or captured by the enemy or close to it."

"I got scared about the chip." My honesty shocked me. "I…"

I stopped speaking in order to hold back tears. I didn't want to have him hear any more vulnerability than I was already showing.

He sighed.

"Generally, I'm able to at least keep track of you."

"I've been hiding in the tunnels."

"Only the tunnels?"

"Well no. I've been elsewhere. Why does it matter?"

"The reception must have been bad."

"Huh?" What the hell is he talking about?

"I'll explain later. You need to come back to me. There's something I need to tell you. You'll be safe with me."

Safe?

I was turning to the one person I'm most conflicted about in the entire world. My heart was fluttering. Part of me wanted nothing more than to reunite with him right then. Give myself to him entirely and let him take care of me. I also feared him. What was done to me and his role in it all. How he was able to mess with my body and mind. Even being away from him still allowed his increasing control over me. I could only escape from this when he lost track of me. Which he somehow had in the last few weeks.

Yet here I was, no longer avoiding him. I was turning to him with nowhere else to go. Letting his claws sink back into me. Returning to the prison he created for me. I couldn't see it, but I felt it.

"Meet me where you drew the woman with the owl."

Athena. He meant Athena.

He hung up. I swiftly left the phone booth.

I only stopped for a moment before returning to him.

***

Athena was in a tunnel under a curved cement bridge. It was a perfect canvas, and I filled it to the brim. It wasn't a place to rest or camp out though; it was too open to the elements. After my work was done I didn't spend too much time there.

But when I was there, I was at least guaranteed to be alone. Unless I'd been followed. Or in this case meeting Aziel.

Vines and moss had grown over part of my work. But the mural was huge and most of the painting was still visible. The setting transitioned from Ocean, to Sky, to Forest. Aphrodite. Amaterasu. Athena. Artemis. All A's. Mostly Greek. An ancestry I didn't have but still longed to be mine. Strength I wanted to be part of me.

My own heritage was rather embarrassing to me. Another reason I was so eager to leave my past behind. But you can't run away from genetics. But you could certainly hide them to an extent.

I had Viking ancestry. I was too pale to pretend I was Greek.

Though most of my own gang found me a sad excuse for them. I was no Viking, they told me. Or I was the saddest excuse for one who ever lived.

I certainly didn't have Gods and Goddesses at my beckon call for assistance.

Did nature hide the higher powers which be in order to help us? Force us to admit our pitfalls and our place before they would appear? Or did they choose to be hidden? In either case it seemed to be if you sought them out, they could be found. At least, that is what people of those ancestry seemed to believe. It seemed to work out for them too.

It was hard to know if such things were even real. I struggled to find them. I had yet to have one come to my aid.

But I hadn't asked either. I was too afraid of not getting any answer to my pleas.

***

Aziel found me quickly. He hair was longer, not unkempt but still wild and earthy. His eyes were fully metallic now. More machine than human.

I would be lying if I said I never had a sex dream about him. Or too many to count after the chip was implanted in me. There was so much mystery to him, I would never be able to get my head around it. I didn't believe he would ever be fully open with me. He'd already kept secrets from me for so long. Why stop now? I was at least hopeful for answers this time. He'd finally end my confusion. My pain. Fill me with....

I stopped the thought.

He was already feeling me with electric currents. I didn't stop him and let the pulsations wash through me. My stomach felt butterflies without the roller coaster sensation. Waves came through my hands and feet. I felt like I could fly. Then he sent a swirling current into me, venturing into my breast and vagina.

"Stop."

He did. Part of me regretted my rejection.

Being around him filled me in a strange way nothing else could. Not even my painting could give me this. Sometimes all I wanted was to be near him. I was too scared to let him in to me fully, but I still felt pleasure from the tendrils of currents which ran between us. I'd shut it off when it went too far. A least, that's what I told myself.

Now I wanted him to touch me. Lightly and softly. Then fully. Let him have every part of me.

Still I resisted. I'd seen how my vulnerability to Conroy had played out. And it wasn't anywhere near as complicated as things were with Aziel.

I knew this frustrated him. Which hurt me somehow.

But I needed to figure out my situation and he was the key. I needed to concentrate.

"How have you been holding up out here?" There was real concern in his voice. Any anger he showed before dissipated.

"Good. Besides the lack of sleeping and showering. And having a lot of people on my tail."

I found my head was shaking before I spoke again. "No, not good actually. I'm not alright. That's why we're talking."

Why I turned myself in.

"Is that the only reason you're coming back?"

"I have nowhere else to go. No family. No friends. The gang hates me. Even though I do missions just as well. Everyone hates me. Even Conroy now. You think I would come back if I had anywhere else to go? Now that I ran off, they're likely to kill me. I broke one of their sacred rules. Turning myself in to them is probably a death sentence. You're all I have."

He smiled, "You won't have to worry about them anymore soon."

"Why? Because you're going to diplomatically fix this? Or are you going to just kill me yourself?

"Why do you think that of me?"

"Then how do you think of me then?" This wasn't the question I should be asking. I still couldn't bring myself to ask about the chip. Lack of sleep was letting my emotions slip.

"You're worth more to me than you know."

I closed the gap between us. The look of surprise was clear on his face. I wrapped my arms around him and sobbed. I was exhausted. All of this was too much. I couldn't handle things. I was finally crumbling. Worn down by the street life. Worn down by my existence.

He returned my embrace and stroked my spine. Those currents were calming me, while his breath on my neck made me ready to let go.

Having felt my thought, his lips were on mine.

He moved my back to the wall. My art was behind me and ahead of him. I breathed as if I was emerging from ice water, taking in sweet oxygen after not being able to find the surface and fearing I'd drown. The sweet relief I found as I reached the surface, knowing I'd live. His mouth was that surface, he breathed air into me. Each gasp and moment I became grateful for.

My inner vibrations continued to increase, especially as his hands moved over my sensitive areas. He pulled off the layers hiding those parts. Fear subsided to longing.

He slowed down to move his hands over all of me, lingering over my womanhood and where I mothered the chip. He pressed his hand over the chip. Sound escaped my mouth and I was brought to ecstasy.

His metallic eyes brighten in satisfaction.

I'm the second human creation to be admired on this wall.

He pushed tightly against me as he kissed my neck and moved his hands to our connecting lover regions. First checking if I'm properly prepared for him and then removing his own layers. Tucking his shirt behind my back to protect me from the concrete wall.

This was only the second man I'd been with and I was surprised how different it felt from the first.

I hung on to him tightly. It had been a while since my last sexual act, so my tightness was apparent. But he worked diligently into me, pinning me with the rest of his body.

Through physical act, there currents running between us intensified. I lost myself in those rushes and waves. Giving and taking of energy. Changing sensations on a whim. Letting us surprise each other in our pleasure. Ensuring climax after climax. Each one with its signature ripple effect which played into the next, while also leaving something else behind. Current layering on current. Pleasure layering on pleasure.

I felt him finish in me. A burst of energy which recharged me. Giving me my power back.

Then I realized he wasn't wearing a condom.

***

Upon coming back to earth, Aziel looked into my eyes stroked my face. He showed gratitude through kissing me on the forehead and lips.

"Aziel…"

"I'm sterile. Both ways." He assured me.

"I'm sorry."

"It was my choice. You're safe with me, don't worry." He kissed me again.

We dressed in silence. My eyes wandered to my work. The colors were brighter to me now. I could even smell the paint. The distinction between the individual colors and the harmony they created together.

I wanted him to do it all to me again, right then. I was ready to give it all back in return. Just to have it all once again.

Aziel was behind me already kissing my neck and lifting my shirt.

Chapter Eighteen

After reaching our currents into each other for hours, we both were finally in a state of exhaustion. He'd fallen asleep against my thigh. I stroked his hair.

This was all wrong. I shouldn't be with him. This was when I should have been making my escape.

I just kept stroking his hair. I was weak. Exhausted from send out every last current of mine. All for the fleeting high of heightened sensation and orgasm.

My eyes looked to the women I'd painted. Wishing I could be more like them. I didn't think I had anything close to their capabilities within me. Or with those who served them. I went from being a pet for one man to another. I craved their approval and desire; whether it was love or not. Even if it would screw me later. This hurt me deeply. I'd never live up to the dreams of my art.

***

"I could really use a burger." Those were his first words upon awakening.

It was too late to run away now. I'd blown my chance.

Beef was a common commodity back in the day. Now cows were few and far between. They'd caused too many environmental issues in the past. The ones that were still around weren't to be eaten. They're living museums. Hamburgers were highly illegal. Even veggies and vegan burgers were often double checked by police to ensure someone wasn't trying to sneak in some beef. But people fantasized about how they would taste all the time. A real old-fashioned burger with fries and a milkshake. Just like back in the 1950s.

"When was the last time you had one?"

"Before my surgery."

This was the most he'd ever told me about himself through words. Perhaps I could finally get answers about the chip. I remained silent though. I realized I was afraid of what the answers would be.

His eyes fluttered, and he fell back to sleep.

I could have tried to run, I had another chance, but I didn't want to anymore.

***

We stayed like that while the sun set and until it rose back up. A clear night made it possible, despite this not normally being a wise rest spot. With Aziel here with me, I knew we'd sense any danger long before it arrived. I'd managed to sleep in that time longer than I had for a while.

When I sensed he was awake, I went to kiss him. He stopped me.

"I have to take care of something."

"What is it?"

"I'll tell you when I return. You need to stay here until I get back."

"Why can't you tell me?"

Aziel ignored the question. "You'll be safe here. Paint if you get bored."

"Why can't you tell me?" I asked again as he walked away. He still didn't answer. Even his thought currents were blocked from me.

I wasn't going to paint over those women. But I could work on the concrete at our feet to experiment on techniques.

No. I deserved answers. He couldn't keep me in the dark like this.

I felt his trail. His concentration on whatever task he was about to undertake would distract him from realizing I was trailing him. I suspected the sex had to do with his lack of sensor.

Once he was way ahead, I started to trail him.

It was about halfway that I realized, he was heading back to our gang's hideout.

Chapter Nineteen

Why was he heading there? Was he going to give me up? Hand me over to the gang for some reward? But why not just drag me over there with him?

My suspicions put me on red alert. But somehow, I knew his intentions weren't to hurt me. He knew bringing me to our old hideout would have put me in grave danger. That's why he didn't want me to follow him.

So, what was he planning then?

Soon I'm hiding in the bushes as he entered the warehouse. Its wrinkled metal coating made it almost gun proof from the outside. There were still no windows, so I couldn't see inside.

I desperately wanted to check on Aziel with my currents. Ensure he was safe. But I feared what would happen if I allowed him to know my location and learned I disobeyed.

Shouting erupted so loud, I could hear them from where I was. But I couldn't understand what they were saying or who they were coming from.

Gun fire and screams erupted from the base. I dropped to the earth as if dodging a bomb, hands over my ears. My whole gang was screaming, except Aziel. He was never a screamer. Conroy gave out a roar as he fought to his very end. There was a chorus of shrills. Some were angry but most were fearful.

I was surrounded by noise. Loud terrifying noise which only grew louder and more chaotic. Machine and man uniting in terrible ways. The sounds of lives ending suddenly and violently. My body was shocked into stillness, as my heart attempted to run away.

Paige Etheridge • 68

I may not have been seeing the face of death. But it was with me. Alongside me, in front of me, touching the deepest parts inside of me.

Violent and deep it still rang hollow. It belonged everywhere, even when we rejected it. Even when we pretended it didn't exist. It was always ready to accept us. Willing to take us whether we felt it timely or not.

Just as suddenly, the base was empty of sound. The silence almost hurt my ears just as much.

I smelled the sandalwood again.

I was being pinned to the earth by strong male hands. Before I could scream, my mouth was covered with tape. The Jackal had found me. I felt how the sun and the earth worked on those hands, as well as metal and plastic. I felt myself becoming bound by him again.

He threw me over his shoulder. I felt my bonds. He'd used the industrial metal rope. To my horror, I realized I wouldn't be able to slip free this time.

I saw we were approaching an armored vehicle. A door opened at the top and another man popped out and pulled me inside. The Jackal stayed right behind me. I felt his hand go under my nose. He was making sure I was breathing. Once he was assured I was alive, he secured me to the wall with straps.

I felt his thumbs wiping at my cheeks. I hadn't realized I'd been crying.

"Knock her out." I heard a voice say.

"I'll sedate her." The voice was slightly musical but firm.

Wait, there was another female here?

A brown-haired woman with a neat bun and honey eyes approached me. She wore green army fatigues and there were smears of face paint. I didn't realize she had a needle until I felt it prick into my skin. I gave a slight wince and exhale. Once she was done, she and the Jackal held my shoulders back.

There was silence except for the wheels of vehicle.
I saw a swirl of muddy colors before I blacked out.

Chapter Twenty

Shining white light filled my eyes and woke me. My vision was blurry. All I could see were black phantoms ahead of me. Silhouettes whose mystery I didn't know housed ally or nightmare. I felt strength and power amongst them, more than I'm used to feeling around people who are supposed to be in charge.

The energy of my gang was ants level compared to the galaxies of power wafting off these individuals.

I saw visions of my life past. My childhood home, being in my room playing amongst my toys, and an old friend I lost years ago. Named after a loving hue. It was only then I realized I was back to dreamland.

***

Darkness lifted. Cold water was poured over my head. I breathed as if I'm breathing for the first time. Hurting as if I was gulping the cold water itself. I was tied up to a metal chair.

The shapes in front of me were still blurry. But they were people for sure. But it was hard to determine if it was few or many.

As my eyes adjusted I realized the face closest to mine was of the Jackal from the fire. The one who kidnapped me. Brought me into this unknown fate. Behind him was a man whose poise told me he was their leader. He was muscular with wild hair tied back. Green eyes watching me without judgement or emotion. My gang knew him as Wild Dog. Rumor was he trained in Africa and earned his name from fighting off, and then befriending, a pack of African Wild Dogs.

"What the hell is going on?" I only had strength to whisper this thought aloud.

"I tracked you using your chip." The Jackal was the one speaking.

"Where are the others?" It was hard to speak. I feared the answer I knew was coming.

"They're all dead. You're the only one left."

Guilt and shock filled me. They hadn't been great to me. They wouldn't have cared if something happened to me. In fact, it was likely they would have killed me themselves. Likely they were planning my execution once they managed to track me down. Though I couldn't know for sure. Conroy was the only one I was ever close to. Even he hadn't really been good to me.

Aziel. My mind whispered. What about him?

Something told me he was alive. A sense of knowing stronger than delusion or denial. Perhaps the chip. But I couldn't trace him. He must had been too far away.

"Can you tell me what happened?"

"No. Not until we've figured it out."

"Was it you and your Jackals? You were the only ones there." I glared into his eyes.

"Don't think you'll believe me even if I say no. We did have orders to kill anyone from your gang on site, since they were quick to kill anyone else. We were tracking just you. The firefight wasn't something we planned. We're not sure what happened. It seemed to have been an inside job. Likely a murder suicide. The drugs for those body prosthetics cause violent behavior. It's a good thing you don't have one."

"You kidnapped and violated me as well?"

"Naomi searched you privately."

"Naomi?"

"The doctor. We needed to ensure you didn't have any other weapons on you. Or the prosthetics."

"Any other weapons?"

"Besides the chip inside you."

"That's a weapon?"

"Naomi is running tests to find out for sure. So far, she's eliminated the possibility you're a robot or clone. Do you not know what it does?"

"Besides moving around what feels like electric currents? I thought that's all it did. Technology doesn't exactly glitch around me though."

I sighed. He tipped his head slightly to the right.

"You're not telling me the whole story."

"I don't know the whole story and that scares me. I didn't want any of this. It was put in me against my will. Now you're telling me I'm some kind of weapon?"

I fought back my tears, but I was sure the Jackal saw them. I was so weak to show him that.

"Maybe Naomi can enlighten you then."

"Is that why you're leaving me alive? Because of the chip?"

"That's not the only reason."

"Why else then?"

"Why did you save my life?"

I didn't answer.

He continued. "You were under strict orders to kill anyone from our army."

"I don't think I have an answer that will satisfy you, besides telling you I'm not a killer."

"So, you were disobeying your gang?"

"I ran away from them. They were likely planning to kill me already even if they hadn't found out about that. I don't think they knew though. They don't exactly track well. Not me at least."

"So, you're not loyal to the gang? That's a first. Conroy made bad leadership choices, but he inspired great loyalty. Still not sure how. We suspect something else was put into those drugs besides keeping the prosthetics from killing the rest of the body."

"They weren't exactly worth being loyal to. Especially after what was done to me."

"So why end up with them in the first place?"

"I didn't have much choice as a child."

"I highly doubt that."

"Enough." Wild Dog said. The Jackal was silenced.

"Why are you making assumptions about my life?"

My visions blurred again. I shook my head. No matter how many times I blinked, it was getting worse. My breathing sped up.

"What's wrong?" I felt the Jackal bringing himself to me.

"I can't see." I felt like I was floating out of my own body.

"Step back and get Naomi." Wild Dog said.

The Jackal left the room.

I started to convulse. Wild Dog quickly brought my chair against the wall and held me there. His swift but firm action assured me.

"Take deep breaths. Naomi is coming."

The Jackal and Naomi entered the room.

"You'll both need to hold her eyes open. She'll be blind permanently if we don't get this in right now."

My panic heightened.

"Keep her breathing."

Each man pried my eyes open. The light hurt my eyes.

Naomi let the drops fall into my eyes.

"Did we get it in time?"

"Her eye color is returning, we got them in time, Indigo. I have to get her unconscious again to ensure nothing else shuts down." I felt a swab of alcohol against my skin and a needle enter my arm again.

Indigo.

How hadn't I realized it before?

My other blue.

I fell into blackness again.

***

I felt my eyes opening but couldn't see.

My hands touched my face. I hit myself to ensure I was truly awake. Fear gripped me. I thought the doctor had saved my sight. What about my painting?

"Your sight will return." Naomi said. She clearly read my frantic body language.

"How can you be sure?"

"It's already improving."

"I can't see."

I heard a clicking of a button. I could see a hint of white light before my eyes.

"You see that I'm sure."

"A bit."

The light went out.

"Your eye function was shut down temporarily by your own body to protect your vision from being permanently damaged. There seemed to be a temporary malfunction in the chip which sent too much electric current to your eyes. The serum calmed this down."

Something wrapped was placed in my hand.

"This is from your pack. Raising your spirits could return your sight faster."

I managed to open the wrapper. First taste told me I was eating a Pop Tart.

"Do you know anyone else with this technology?"

"There's a man named Aziel who seems to know how to get electrical reactions out of it and me."

"Perhaps he is holding the same technology as well."

The thought hadn't crossed my mind. Was it possible? Is that why I felt such a strong connection to him? How he was able to charge me? Looking back, it seemed obvious though.

"When you're done eating, I need to run some test. There are things I can only test for now that you're awake."

"Such as?"

"If the chip is about to shut down the rest of your body."

Chapter Twenty-One

For a moment I choked on crust and sweet filling.

"It's not happening right now. But it may be soon. No reason not to finish the Pop Tart."

I ate the rest slowly.

"We'll be shifting your diet to prepare you. Ideally, I'd like some more weight on you before having to do anything too intrusive. There's been a lack of nutrients in your diet for years. You should have osteoporosis by now. But it seems the chip may have saved your bones."

"So, the chip is helping me?"

"It's more complicated than that. The chip seems to be acting on parts of the body which will improve it as a conduit point. While having lesser influence on parts which would be too vulnerable."

"Bones can conduct electricity?"

"No. Most of your electrical movement is through your nerves and blood. But the bones provide stability and mobile ions. Your skin has been producing extra oil to better conduct as well."

I debated asking for the Snickers bar. I was feeling my hunger.

"Your body seems to be producing its own electricity, originating from the chip. This is also causing damage to your cells. Parts are dying off and being replaced with something else. The nerves are mutating entirely."

"What about my brain?" The question popped out of my mouth.

"The conduits seem to be improving brain function for the most part. But this and your heart are your areas at highest risk."

"Why is that?"

"The electric charge is increasing in your body. In time it will likely become too much for the cells which haven't adapted in the same way, to fail. The heart and brain functions couldn't be changed by your chip or you would die. But the behavior of the chip increasing charge seems to be overriding its smart cell function. Either your brain will fry, or your heart will suffer fatal cardiac arrest."

I wasn't hungry anymore.

***

The next few weeks were a blur of unseen tests and preparations.

I'm fed better than I'd eaten in years. For a long time, berries, oysters, and salmon were all novelties which were simply out of reach for me. Being part of my gang, you don't get to eat too well. Conroy was paranoid the local foods were poisoned by the government. We were only allowed to eat approved rations. Sometimes there would be a lot of food stolen in bulk, but most of it was canned and processed. Most of the food was gross, hence why I didn't eat much of it. Being on the run made my meal prospects even worse.

Naomi allowed me the occasional bits of chocolate. I'm told they're European. Helped keep spirits up amongst the army ranks. It felt almost like coffee on the tongue with its richness. Lingering in the mouth like a ballerina dancer.

Naomi often smelled of coffee and chocolate when the medical scent didn't take over. She offered me her coffee in appropriate doses. I felt cheated of so many things which should had been in my life before. But at least I was enjoying them now. On some level, I also enjoyed all the care and attention. Even if there was a ton of uncomfortable tests. She checked places which made me wonder about her methods and took questionably large quantities of my blood.

Wild Dog occasionally broke our solitude to ask for reports. They spoke a language to each other I wasn't familiar with. Naomi later told me it was Afrikaans.

"What are you not telling me?" I asked.

"Our language is a way to remain connected to where we spent much of our lives. That's something Wild Dog and I share. I like to be open with my patients. It ensures treatment goes more smoothly. But there are also things happening within our army that I'm not authorized to tell you. But medically, I've been telling you everything I know for sure."

"Are you from Africa?"

"Wild Dog is. He learned to fight there and recruited most of his army there. I'm not. I went in attempts to stop the prosthetics and drug epidemic in South Africa. Africa changed a lot after the blood diamond business ended. I thought I'd be able to heal people of everything else. No doctor can do that. Eventually the disease was turning my patients against me. The only reason I'm alive is because of Wild Dog. I accepted my defeat in trying to save the world and joined Wild Dog's army. I attempt to aid and save one life at a time now."

Diamonds were available in abundance nowadays. There was always a lot of them, but the last companies who kept them hidden away and jacked up the prices were killed off by the drug epidemic and the people of Africa. Now people added permanent diamonds to their bodies. Noses, fingers, toes, anywhere which they could be imbedded. They'd become more popular than body piercings. Most got the plain white ones. Some people had theirs dyed before implant. Some people just want to be a sparkling rainbow against all this grit. I guessed it helped people feel more natural in their unnatural world, having shiny rocks embedded inside them. Having their bodies carry pieces of Earth.

I never desired to have it, or any kind of implant for that matter.

I wondered how Indigo gotten involved in this army. He never seemed to be the war type to me. Was he ever even in Africa? Then again, last I saw him we were children. How much could I know someone at that point?

I didn't see Indigo during those few weeks. I didn't ask about him either.

***

My sight started to break through the darkness. At first, I saw in purples, greys, and blacks. Then I saw my favorite color again. That's when much of my joy returned. Naomi noticed a drastic progress in my healing afterward.

She offered me books, which I eagerly read at night.

My nails were now shiny without chips or breaks. It was weird seeing my naked nails like this. I had been embarrassed about my nails, always damaged from my lifestyle. Now they were actually beautiful.

Slowly over the next few days the rest of my world turned on the rest of its colors. The richness of yellows, pinks, red, and orange. Even green and brown. I vowed two things: to never take my sight for granted and to paint when the first opportunity presented itself.

***

I asked Naomi if I could see myself in the mirror, since it had been weeks since I'd seen my own face. Yet I was scared to look at myself. Naomi put up a tiny mirror with an unbreakable design in the bathroom part of her medical wing.

Wild Dog entered for a report. She excused herself.

Alone for the first time in weeks, I finally approach the mirror.

I saw the blue in my hair was down to my tips. My blonde was returning. My skin was clear. For the first time in my entire life, I looked bright and clean. I touched the image before me. Was this girl really me?

Indigo appears next to my reflection.

"My blue is disappearing." I said.

"Not where it matters."

I turned to him. Indigo was much taller than when I last saw him. My head made it to his shoulder. He wasn't so skinny either, he'd built up some muscle. His hair was still long dark and curly. He wasn't quite so pale now. But his eyes still held all those purply wonders.

I had so many questions I wanted to ask him.

Suddenly his facial expression changed.

"What is it?"

"Look at your face again."

To my horror, my reflection revealed my skin was turning blue. I collapsed.

"Naomi!" Indigo shouted. He'd managed to catch me before I hit the ground.

"What's happening?" I asked.

I looked at my hand again. I'd never been terrified in my life seeing so much of my favorite color. I felt electrical discharge in my body. I felt fireworks of electrical sparks flare in random parts of my body. My vision was turning black and purple again.

Wild Dog rushed to us.

"Naomi is preparing for surgery. We need to get the chip out of her now."

Chapter Twenty-Two

Wild Dog and Indigo carried me to the operating table. Naomi was already gloved with materials at hand.

"We might already be too late. But most likely, we have just enough time to get it out."

At least Naomi was honest.

"I'm staying." Indigo said to Wild Dog.

"Fine." He replied.

"Sky's blood is in the back over there. Get it out and ready for me."

Indigo obeyed.

"We're not going to have time to knock her out. I can't get her my anesthetics, or the chip could over respond and kill her." Indigo was by our side again "Hold her down for me, both of you."

I felt a swab of alcohol across my belly.

"Sky, I'm sorry. You can get through this." She tied something into my mouth. "Bite on to this. Try not to look."

The human body wasn't designed for this. It wasn't meant to be opened. If it was, it meant it was being eaten by a predator and death was on the horizon. I was going to die right here and now.

Stop it Sky, I told myself. I could get through this.

"Talk to her." Naomi said.

"I don't know what to say." Indigo responded.

The cut into my navel didn't hurt as much as I expected. After all, I had tried to remove the chip myself. I did get a sense of an out of body experience. Perhaps that's why it hurt less. Indigo pressed into me harder as it happened, but Wild Dog maintained the same pressure.

"Just be encouraging then. I'm going in."

Indigo hesitated. Color was returning to my vision.

I peeked at the surgery. Seeing all that red, things were suddenly more painful. I looked away again.

"Look up and count the stars with me." My responding laugh hurt a bit and was muffled by whatever was in my mouth. We used to sneak out at night together. Laying on a grassy hill, we'd attempt to count all the stars in the sky. We never managed to finish before falling asleep.

"1...2...3…" We counted together. Him through words and me with quick hums. I imagined the stars above us, and not the white ceiling blocking the view.

"Can you remove the roots?" Wild Dog said.

"No need. The roots of the chip are retracting on their own. I'm going to be able to remove this more easily than expected. It's coming out now."

I felt the chip leaving my body. Current came up to meet it but stopped once Naomi placed it on the table next to us. I was seeing it for the first time. The surface was smooth with a perfect circular hole cut in the middle. It was square and blue. Conroy was right, I'd been filled with more blue. It was see-through in a way. I could see there was current still moving around in the chip itself. I could still feel the chip too. My own blood was still on it, but the roots weren't visible anymore. How could it be?

That thing didn't belong in me, but it had been a part of me over the course of these few months. Or had it been a full year? I didn't have a good sense of time anymore. Before I'd feared I would have to live with it forever. Now I was finally free of it.

Naomi was stitching me up when the lights went out.

Naomi screamed. I felt Wild Dog let go of me and run to her aide.

The chip was now sending out shocks of blue through the whole room.

Darkness consumed me again.

Chapter Twenty-Three

I awakened to see Indigo sitting next to me. I was still in bed in the medical wing. On the table next to me, were the blue chocolates I'd loved since I was a child. Shaped like sea stars with a sapphire like center. I watched the light reflection change as I moved it around in the sun. The arms had an edible sparkle as well. It was one of the few girly things I allowed myself. Especially since it was blue. I never ate the pink ones.

They were made from a plant which had been a cross between blueberry and cacao. The result was one of the most wonderful man made treats I'd ever tasted. Now I was still watching them in the artificial light before I ate them. They shone beautifully, even without the real sun. But I wanted to see them in real solar light again.

Fruit and chocolate swirled in my mouth. I took another.

"Didn't realize these were still made."

"They're quite popular actually. But only specialty shops carry them."

Made sense. A street rat like me wouldn't have access to them.

"Thank you." I caught the first smile I had seen from him since our reunion.

I caught a whiff and saw the blue rose bouquet in water on the table next to me. The sensations brought me a sense of peace.

He still remembered so much about me.

Blue roses. Was he the one leaving them at my grave?

He leaned into me.

"How are you feeling?"

"I'm enjoying this."

I put the chocolates down. I wanted to save some for later, as hard as it was to do so. I spied the white scar below my navel. I remembered why I was here. Trapped in yet another medical facility recovering from yet another surgery.

I felt the absence of the chip fully now. There weren't any more currents moving within me.

"I thought I'd be relieved to have that out of me. But now, I'm not sure how I feel."

"That's understandable."

"Is it?"

"Yeah."

"Did you figure out what it's for, now that it's out of me?"

"We're still trying to figure out what that thing does."

Then I remembered what happened before I blacked out.

"What happened to the others?"

"That light show caused some freaky hallucinations and physical reactions. Naomi got the worst of it. I had some issues as well. Wild Dog didn't have any problems though. He was able to get us all back to normal. I'm still not sure how, but I'm glad he learned a thing or two from Naomi. We're theorizing it has to do with the metal implants in his head which made him immune."

"How is she?"

"Naomi is taking some time to herself. Apparently, she was reliving something which happened to her in Africa. Wild Dog recognized what was happening since he was the one who got her out of there at the time."

"And you?"

He didn't answer. But his face told me he returned to something as well.

"I'm so sorry."

"It didn't affect you on the way out. Test confirmed that. There was fear the surgery would kill you through the release of toxins or shocks. Or your body going into shock after having the chip removed. But test after test showed you're fine."

"Where is it now? It's not too far away, is it?" I still felt like I had a sense of where it was. To the north of me.

Indigo followed my eyes. He knew I could feel where it was.

"The chip is being contained in a vault which absorbs the electricity as it's analyzed. Though it seemed to be shut off now that it is no longer in you. Hibernating. Or perhaps even dying itself."

"It's not dying. It's hibernating. I can still feel it."

I ran my hand where the chip had been. No bump this time. I couldn't feel the stitching either. Just a slight line in my skin.

The pain was different this time. I didn't feel the soreness I should have considering the surgery. I didn't feel my skin's cries of discomfort being ripped apart and having to find its way back together once again. Perhaps it was following the routine from before, from being opened and closed previously, so my body wasn't in shock this time.

Relief hadn't arrived. I wasn't sure if it was coming.

Indigo reached out to stop my hand, slightly brushing my scar. I looked at him. It felt different. Not like when Aziel would touch me there. It was surprisingly normal. Ticklish and a bit warm. The feeling shocked me in how ordinary it was. He lowered his hand.

"Sorry. You're still healing. You know what they say about touching stitches."

"I don't see any."

"Oh. I guess Naomi used that trick of hers. They're there for sure. Just invisible."

"I touched them last time and I'm still alive."

His face changed. I felt mine shift in turn.

"I never knew why I was chosen." I looked away.

"This shouldn't have happened to you."

Silence flowed between us for a while. I let it provide its comfort.

"Do you remember how I got my name?" Indigo asked.

I nodded. Finally, we were admitting to our history.

"You said I was your favorite person in the world. Since blue was your favorite color, you wanted to name me after a shade which lies next to blue on the rainbow. You would be blue, and I would be indigo."

I remembered the story. His eyes had a beautiful mutation similar to mine. Blue with purple elements swirling inside. That's why I had named him as I did; his eyes were truly indigo. Those eyes always enchanted me. Made me believe in things which couldn't be real.

"How did you know it was me?"

"Your eyes are the same. You were reported dead years ago. At first, I wasn't sure if you were a twin, a clone, a robot, or even just a girl with similar genetics. A vivid hallucination and even the possibility of a ghost crossed my mind. But your eyes. There is nothing which could have been faked by that. You were very much alive."

"Eyes are one of those things which can easily be changed."

"Not the type of blue you have. A mutation of the HERC2 as well as influence of SLC24A4 and TYR influence the creation of blue eyes. But I have yet to see a genetic code or a lab able to create all the shades of blue I find in yours. They still haven't found the code which makes eyes like yours and mine. Your eyes, as well as other parts about you, are still a mystery to modern science. So when I saw that sapphire, navy, turquoise, aqua and sky blend…"

He paused. Hearing him say my chosen name after all this time gave me a funny feeling inside. I was still Keira at the time, but he called me Sky since that's what I wanted.

"I knew it had to be you. Though I'm not sure how you faked your death. That skull fragment..."

"Was recreated using my DNA. They extract a few cells of bone, which hurt like a bitch by the way, via needle and made the cells reproduce around a curved shape until they had the shape of a skull fragment. They shaved a bit off to make it jagged. Then they took it into a field and one of the gang members called it in anonymously."

Indigo's eyebrows lowered, and his eyes met the ground.

"I used to leave flowers on your grave. Blue roses. I knew you loved those. They're not of this world, just like you. It was revealed to the public later that strain had been developed on Mars and brought back to Earth since it would fetch a high price. But it grew like a bamboo forest, no one was able to stop it. And no one was willing to put a price on it anymore either. I was angry you didn't get the chance to flourish in the same way."

Hearing him talk about his feelings was making me rather uncomfortable. The last and only person to be fully honest with me like this had been him. I'd enjoyed it at the time. Now, after years of reading into what people were saying and dealing with the frustrations of a lack of communication, I didn't know how I felt about this. Years of wanting truth, and I was still more comfortable with lies.

"I never felt you were there at your grave though. No matter how much I wanted to feel you, or how hard I wanted to believe, I never felt you there. I just thought Heaven might have been a lie. But now I know why, you were still of this Earth."

"My survival depended on the world thinking I was dead." I said.

Indigo's breathing grew heavy. His eyes met mine again.

"That was a really fucked up thing that you did. Pretending you were dead. Do you know what it's like to mourn someone? I thought you'd been murdered. I even went searching for your killer. I wanted them to pay. I dreamed about killing them. Giving them the most painful end known to man. My thirst for revenge drove me day after day. Yet I hit dead end after dead end when looking for who ended you. There simply wasn't anything. And it had all been because you weren't murdered at all. I spent most of my life hating someone who wasn't even real, who never committed the crime I hated them for."

"That's why you thought about shooting me yourself when you first saw me?"

"I needed to act once I realized what gang you were part of. But I wasn't planning on shooting unless I had to. Guns are a deterrent as well. Not just a killing tool. Once I saw your eyes I knew it was you."

"Still don't appreciate you pointing a gun in my face." My jaw tensed.

"Why didn't you tell me you were alive? I spent all this time thinking you were dead. Thinking I let some murderer and rapist have his way with you. Thinking I'd failed you." Those last words lost the intensity of the others.

"You were a kid. What good could you have done for me?" My voice rose.

"I joined this army after you left. Hoping to get past your death. Hoping to find your killer. They have more resources than regular civilians. I thought they'd make me strong and savvy enough to finally connect the dots and have my revenge. But there was a heavy price to pay in return. Still I thought it would lead me to avenging you. Until eventually I saw your blue eyes out of the fire staring back into mine."

"You're pinning your choices on me?"

"I only joined because of you."

"I didn't tell you to join the army. If you regret your decision, then quit."

"No. I wouldn't now, even if I could."

"Why not? Perhaps it hasn't ruined your life after all."

"It's not about that. It's about serving the higher cause."

"Conroy said something similar in his mantra."

"Conroy was just trying to control all of you for his own gain."

"And the military doesn't?"

"We're an army outside of the traditional military."

"You still need the mindset to follow orders of one man. Be efficient at killing whoever your superiors set to die."

"Our cause is greater."

"Who's to judge that? We're all pitiful humans at the end of the day. We're a small play in the infinite workings of a random universe. I don't even know what you guys do. I'm hidden in Naomi's wing. How many have you killed for that cause?"

"Our workings are confidential from you as of right now. I, we, don't even know if we can trust you.'"

I assumed as much.

"How can I even trust you then?"

"You can trust me with your life."

"Since I saved yours?"

"Since I still feel the same for you I always have."

"Which is being inspired to kill in my name? How romantic. I'm sure that works well for your occupation."

"I haven't needed to kill anyone for you it turns out."

"How about my gang? Or were you disappointed that someone else got to them before you did? Or are you lying to me?"

"I have yet to lie to you and I'm not going to start to now. I can't say the same for you."

"I lied to stay alive. I doubted anyone would miss me. For a long time, it didn't seem anyone did."

"How could you not know how I felt? That this would hurt me?" He let a flicker of sorrow show in the blue of his eyes before hues of anger took back over.

"How many childhood friendships have come and gone without even an afterthought? I assumed I would be the same for you."

"You weren't. The day it was presumed you were dead, I died too."

"So, who am I speaking to now?"

"The man I became in his place.

"I didn't kill the little boy inside you. You did. You joined to find a killer, and a killer was inside you all along."

Indigo clenched his fist. He took a deep breath. His body remained tense.

"You're still trying to be my knight in shining armor. You couldn't save me back then. And I doubt you'll be able to save me now."

"I'm just doing now what I couldn't for you as a child. Save you from yourself. Protect you for those looking to use you."

"So now you and the army will use me instead. Your army will use me as a guinea pig. Likely using me to create new weapons. You will use me to band aid your emasculation. You said it yourself, you're not the same person anymore. You serve them first and foremost now. If that includes needing to kill me, then you'll have to do it. Which as much as I don't want to believe it, is likely now that the chip has been removed."

"I wouldn't." The hesitation in his voice was apparent.

"You won't know until you have to make the choice. Though it would be an ironic end, wouldn't it? You actually becoming my killer." I looked away. I was suddenly nauseous.

Indigo exited the room.

Hiding into my knees I began to sob. The bed below me creaked as if tattle telling of my sorrow.

***

I dreamed I was swimming in an ocean. I was breathing underwater somehow. I was surrounded by shades of ocean blue. I felt currents move through me and around me. Sometimes they hurt. But mostly they were comforting. They were sending me to a destination I knew nothing of. Orcas joined me. I was overjoyed. I'd never seen anything like it before, except in photographs, and now they were right here protecting me.

I soon realized some of them were cyborgs. A goggled eye on one. A robotic tail on another. Robotic fins here and there. Had they done this to survive? Or was this done to them and they survived despite it?

As we swam along, I no longer could tell the difference between the natural ones and the altered ones. My vision no longer told me. Not even my intuition. At first this scared me. I didn't know what to make of it. But I realized it didn't matter. They belonged with each other and I belonged among them.

When I awoke I couldn't figure out what the dream meant, if anything.

Something inside told me it did, this frightened me.

***

Wild Dog came to my room the next day.

"It seems that you're healing well."

"Yeah." I slowly picked at the chocolates from yesterday.

"It's time to tell you what's going to happen next."

I'm silent. Wild Dog filled the pause.

"You're being moved to the all-women's army. They're known as Infinity. We've kept your presence a secret up until the removal of the chip. After that, we were no longer able to do so. The men here are suspicious of you. Your previous gang affiliation as well as the experimentation done on you is turning you into a target amongst my men. Despite your rescue of Indigo. To keep our operations moving smoothly and efficiently, as well as for your own safety, it's best to send you to our allies."

I hadn't heard of Infinity or an all-women's army. It was hard for me to wrap my head around the concept.

"So, no chance to experiment on me, huh? I was wondering why I hadn't met your other men."

"A few of my men were part of the operation to retrieve you. They were sworn to secrecy, up until your chip was removed and where you were being placed was sorted. Keeping you away from my men was for their safety rather than yours."

I decided to ignore what I wanted to respond to that last statement.

"So now what?"

"Naomi will be going with you to ensure you're not a threat to others or yourself. She'll still need to run more tests on you. It's unclear what lasting influence the technology had on you."

"So, you can't just let me go?"

"No."

"What about the chip?"

"That will remain with us."

"So what else happens to me now?"

"This is a chance to prove your allegiance and that you're no longer a danger. Naomi will have you cleared within the next few days. You can do the rest of your healing while you're with Infinity. Naomi will fill you in on everything else."

"What about Indigo?" I couldn't believe what I said.

"What about him?"

"Nothing. Sorry."

"I'll see you off when you leave."

With that, Wild Dog exited the room.

I didn't want those chocolates anymore.

***

It's Indigo, not Naomi, who arrived next.

Once the door closes behind him, I started screaming.

"What the hell is this? I can't handle being in an army!"

"We don't have a choice."

"There's really nothing you can do for me?"

"This is something I'm doing for you."

"What? What kind of favor is this? How about having them let me go?"

"You know that's not possible."

"Then send me to some work camp. I don't know. Something else."

"There's no one else who can handle you in the event you prove to be a danger but will also not take advantage of you."

"Do you really see me as a threat?"

"It's what the chip did to you, rather than your gang affiliation, that is the problem. Your body sent out that blast after the operation, not that chip."

I leaned back against the wall.

"Protecting me by forcing me to fight. I was safer when I was still living on the street."

"Is that what you really want? Do you see no other value to your life? I never understood why you ran away to that world."

"I didn't have to worry about becoming a killer like you."

Indigo's eyes brightened into purple fire.

"You'll end up under the hands of yet another gang. I won't let that happen to you. I'm not going to fail you again."

"You feel like you need to babysit me? And you don't care about me having to kill just like you? Or better yet, if I'm killed under your supervision, that's still an improvement."

"Nothing is going to happen to you like that."

"I'm considered dangerous, aren't I? You can't predict what those people will do in that army over there! All over something I had no say in!"

"The gang you were involved with killed many. You being involved with them was your decision. Which understandably is going to make people not trust you. Add in your relationship with the chip and there's assumptions you could seek revenge for your fallen comrades. Or even just use your abilities for destruction for your own gain."

"They were no comrades of mine. I have no interest in being a weapon for the Jackal, Infinity, you, or anyone else."

"You'll need to prove that. Infinity is that chance."

"You're lying to me just like everyone else in my life. Just like Conroy. Just like Aziel. Just like my parents. You're no better than any of them."

"You're the one lying to yourself."

"You just want another chance. That's what this is really about. What, you were going to be able to save us both all those years ago? Live off the land? Run off into the forest and make some fairy tale? Or what was that crazy plan you had. I don't remember. We were kids. Young and stupid. Especially you. You drew those dreams with your own hand to make them seem more real to you. I at least learned quickly dreams aren't worth having."

"You know those are lies too."

"Not the dreams you had! You seem to have maintained some grand design for my life. Against my will."

"While your choices have gotten you in more danger as the years progress. Luckily for you, those choices have been taken away from you."

"What else was I supposed to do at the time? I had no family to support me. No way to better myself. What resources and choices did I have? I choose the only path which was laid before me. And I just kept going."

"You had me."

"What does that mean?"

"You've always had me. And it you threw that away. I keep finding myself coming back to you for some reason. I still find you worth it. That should mean something to you."

"Feeling emasculated because I saved you? You couldn't save me back then and you couldn't save yourself. You can't save me now. You're just trying to save me so that you feel like a man again."

"That's not the reason. You can't blame me caring on some manhood issue. You're more than that. I see a lot in you. All the things I saw back then. You're clearly not seeing it the same way in yourself. Even if you know you're not completely helpless."

"Well my life has always been controlled regardless. It won't be any different now."

"Things will finally get better."

"Because you'll have power over me?"

"You'll be given power back when you're finally responsible to use it."

"You're not the only one who thought they knew best for me and looked to control me. But you were the first. I've been trapped in that cycle ever since."

"I'm not going with you, Sky. I didn't plan on it. You'll have to shine through all your own. And I won't have any power over you. But perhaps you can find your own and make good use of it."

He left me alone to my thoughts.

***

Even as a child, Indigo seemed to be on a great mission in life. To make the world better. To fight off the powers making it harder for everyone. Rebalance the natural world and the electronic one.

For him, I was part of it all. His mission always started with saving me. I think he thought it was a starting point, if he could save me, he could do everything else he wanted to do. Now I saw him being unable to save me at the time, brought him to where he was now. But he was still looking to save the world.

Me? I just wanted to survive it. Everything I did was based on survival. Perhaps greater ambition would have served me better. Or I may have just been trapped in yet another man-made cage. Be it army, a regular job, jail….

We'd both been down such different roads. Yet all of our choices somehow brought us back together again. I had no explanation.

But as always, I was still in danger.

I could prove I felt nothing for my gang. But it was possible my lack of allegiance would make me even more dangerous. Might make me more unpredictable. Especially with whatever the chip had done to my body.

It could be decided ending me would be better for everyone, just in case. Indigo wasn't understanding that.

Doing a good job in my gang got me nothing but shit. How would this be any different?

I didn't owe him anything. Despite whatever weird cocktail of feelings between reminiscence, betrayal, relief, and redemption he or I felt. I didn't owe his damn army anything either. Or the new one I was being forced into.

I'd need to find a way to escape once again.

Chapter Twenty-Four

As I sat on the cool metal table, Naomi performed her last round of tests and spoke to me about what to expect from the women's army. They trained in nature-based environments using ancient fighting techniques. They used newer technology as well.

They weren't interested in being my babysitters. I was expected to train and work hard. If I refused, it was likely I was going to be killed. Failure wasn't going to be much of an option for me.

Becoming a weapon or death were my only options for them apparently.

I wanted a mental break.

"Can we switch gears for a moment?"

"Sure. Any symptoms on your end or is there something else happening you want me to look at?"

"Naomi? Were you ever involved with Wild Dog?"

"What do you mean?"

"Like romantically or sexually?"

She blushed.

I rushed my next words. "I'm sorry if I made you uncomfortable. I've just been wondering since you both seem to have something, but I can't see what it is. It's not my business really. I can change topic again if you want."

"It wouldn't work between us." Naomi turned her head to the right. That hadn't been the answer I anticipated. Especially with its honesty.

"Why not?"

"He's in love with war. He doesn't have room to love a woman. I also suspect he would be more into men even if there was room for someone."

"And you?"

"I'd rather not be intimate with anyone. It makes things too messy." Her eyes were looking at the floor.

"I can relate to that."

"Sky." Naomi was looking me in the eyes again. Her honey eyes were shining, and it made me smile for a moment. She placed her hands over mine, which were crossed over my legs. She leaned in closer to me.

"I know you've been dealing with a lot. Your whole life has been difficult and the situation you're in now poses challenges you've yet to face. But I'm not just here just to study you. As my patient, as your friend, I want to help you get through this."

"Why? So, you all can use me as a weapon?" She hadn't been the target for my anger yet. But I felt it coming on.

"You'll have the chance to be free again if all goes well." She cooled me down fast.

"Really?" I was embarrassed how easily my excitement showed.

"There's a good chance the chip didn't have any permanent alterations on your body. We'll know for sure within the next year. If that's the case, we can continue studying the chip and you'll be able to go."

"What about the charge my body released after surgery?"

"It may have been one last aftershock from the chip. We'll know for sure soon."

"What about Indigo?"

"What about him?"

"He can't force me to stay, right?"

"No. He's not of high enough ranking to make a call like that. So, let me ask you something now, what has your involvement been with him previously? Wild Dog was keeping Indigo away from you because he sensed a history between you two. He feared it would cloud Indigo's judgement."

"Childhood friends."

"Nothing more?"

"I hadn't seen him since I was thirteen. There wasn't a chance for a lot to happen."

"Evidence points otherwise."

"Fine. He was my only real friend in my entire life. I still thought about him a lot over the years too. Seems he still cares about me. But the feelings are complicated between us."

Why was I being so honest?

"I see."

"Wait. What do you mean Wild Dog was keeping Indigo away from me?"

"Indigo is one of his best men. Everything you could want in a fighter. He didn't break under interrogation or being surrounded by the enemy. But Wild Dog noticed you caused a reaction in Indigo he never saw in him before."

"Oh."

"I've said too much."

"It's fine. Indigo is more loyal to your army now than anything. If you need me destroyed, he'd be willing to pull the trigger."

"That won't be necessary."

***

This was my last night alone before I'd be picked up by Infinity. Who they were and what they stood for were still mysteries to me, despite Naomi's explanation.

I'd finally been given my backpack back. It was a comfort seeing my own things. Seeing my paints even if I couldn't use them at the moment. The dream catcher and stuffed unicorn I always kept stashed away. I wasn't eagerly noshing on all my goodies as I'd previously fantasized about. Good nutrition changed your appetite. Still, I took comfort in the Arizona Iced Tea and Snickers while I listened to the rain.

Was this my life? Simply being shifted for a group's prerogative, one after the other? Until their causes killed me?

Why keep living? What point was there? Even if and when I managed to escape, wouldn't I just be scooped up by yet another more powerful force? Only this time, I could also be a powerful bioweapon. Used to win wars. Used to end lives.

I shuddered at the thoughts.

I didn't feel like a weapon. Since the chip was removed, I hadn't felt currents riding through me like I use to. I missed it in a way. I even missed the chip.

I felt the spot where it had been. My body felt hollow there now. A phantom pain where it should have been. Like still feeling your fingers moving when your hand was removed years ago. In all of this, I felt I lost a part of myself. Be it an artificial part. But now, it was so real to me and who I was. I didn't know who I was without it.

Aziel crossed my mind for the first time since just after I was put into the armored vehicle.

Did he have the chip? Was his also removed? Then where did his powers come from? Perhaps his hadn't tried to kill him yet. Or wouldn't at all. Or would in the future. For now, I knew he was still alive. I imagined him near water. But I couldn't feel anything else. Perhaps our connection had dimmed forever. Perhaps I was finally safe from him.

Yet there were so many things I still wanted to ask him. Questions Naomi couldn't answer, and I wasn't sure ever could despite her best effort. I wanted to know if he faced the same identity crisis as I. Having been altered so much by technology, how had he reconciled who he was?

Did others try to use him? Or was he now using the technology only for himself?

Then there were the questions which filled me with anger and sadness. Why drag me into it? Why make me suffer as he had? Why do this to me against my will? Why not tell me what I needed and longed to know? Why not help me understand?

Despite missing the chip, I still wished it never been in me. I wouldn't have been so conflicted and confused. Or dangerous. It was possible his decision was going to cost me my life.

Were there any choices I could make which would keep me alive?

I let my thoughts go to the rain.

Chapter Twenty-Five

Morning came, and Naomi woke me. I was already packed. So was she. Since we were heading into the wilderness, she was limited in what she could bring. She managed to fit a ton of solar powered equipment into one suitcase. I was impressed. Wild Dog escorted us outside. This was the first time I'd been outside of the building since I came. Grass was beneath my feet. A beautiful blue sky above. Ahead was the deep dense forest, from which came the sounds of strolling hoofs.

In the distance, figures emerged from the woods. Two women on horseback; one black stallion and the other white.

Their armor showed off their figures in the greens and gold knots which traced them. I couldn't believe built bodies like that could be real. I wasn't used to seeing women so muscular and yet feminine. They still held so much grace and beauty. I spied echo guns. High end technology. But I also saw they each had swords and short knives.

I couldn't fathom they were of a real army. This was a technological age. Not an age for ancient warfare tactics. Or old-fashioned weapons. Or philosophies and warfare theory that's thousands of years old. But then again, what did I know about combat? It's not like I ever ran an army. Or was ever fighting in one. All I had was the street and the gang. The wars I fought were about survival.

These people were so different than the ones I'm used to.

"Andromeda. Clete. It's been some time." Wild Dog smiled for the first time in front of me.

The women contrasting each other like day and night. Andromeda's hair reminded me of the rising sun, orange and illuminating. It moved in waves just like a flame would. Her eyes were emerald green. White skin, but without a single freckle. Clete's hair was shadow black. Her silver eyes cut through the air and reminded me of both an owl and the moon. Yet she was also pale.

Andromeda smiled in turn.

"Our last encounter was the galactic battle, wasn't it?"

"Yes."

"You once again proved yourself a valiant hero."

"As did you."

Naomi lowered her eyes.

"You're the good doctor?"

"Yes." Naomi said quickly and quietly. Her eyes met Andromeda's.

"Pleasure. Wild Dog has spoken highly of your skill. It will be nice to steal your abilities for however long we can have you."

"I'm happy to fulfill my duties." Her body almost seemed to bow a bit.

Clete got off her horse to inspect me. She lifted my arms and rolled her eyes.

"Puny." Her voice is deep and piercing as a falcon.

She pulled out her sword and aimed it at my breast.

"You prove a threat to us, and we'll destroy you."

"That's enough, Clete." Andromeda said.

I stared Clete right into those silver eyes and pushed myself into the blade.

She retracted her sword.

"Courage will more than make up for that in the meantime," Clete turned her head to Andromeda, "She's going to need a lot of work."

"You did too, if you don't remember." Andromeda said.

Andromeda threw me on her white horse. Wild Dog guided Naomi onto Clete's horse.

"I'll see you soon." He said to Naomi.

"Soon." She replied in turn.

Their eye contact lasted until Andromeda ordered her horse forward, and Clete's followed in turn.

I watched Wild Dog until the deepening woods complete blocked him out. He was watching Naomi. I didn't see what she did in turn.

***

As we treaded deeper into the forest, Andromeda's and Clete's armor seemed to blend in better with surrounding wood, turning a brown color. Was it designed that way? I asked Andromeda about it. She responded that their armor changed tones automatically based on their thought process. Whether it was to stand out in an open field to blind the enemy or better conceal themselves in the wilderness when plotting an ambush. Their armor could mimic the color of snow or the night sky itself. Or emit a light all its own.

The smells of the deep wood which surround us were so overwhelming. It's wetness. It's abundance. The way the rain left behind a hyperrealism to all those shades of green. Here and there I would see a falcon. Or a fox. Perhaps even a wolf. I couldn't help but be in awe.

What I'm used to is a metal jungle. Cracks of concrete to hide between. Walls to tag my art, make some meaning out of my existence. Broken buildings to temporarily take shelter. Streets to lead me occasionally to safety but mostly to nowhere. Technological gadgets to make things easier or harder along the way.

But these woods? I've seen them from the outside and wondered what that world was like. Being inside now, I felt something so old, something so alien to me but such a part to who I was. A part of myself I'd been ignoring my whole life.

Night falls. The sounds of owls were louder than I'd ever heard before.

In between my short stints of falling asleep as we continued to ride, I had short dreams. Of a crescent moon appearing on Clete's horse's head and lighting the way. Of coffee forming itself within a jack-o-lantern. Flashes of Indigo. The sounds surrounding us would play into these short dreams too. Flashes of the horrors I feared were in these woods would manifest there.

Not once did either rider flinch. Naomi seemed alert but not overly fearful.

We continued navigating the paths in the dark. How did those two know the way to wherever we were going? Then I noticed they were looking up to the sky. Tracking based on the stars. That's their map. The moon, their compass, showing them the way. They'd look to the forest around them for important landmarks to assure them we're on the right track. Though the stars remained their most important guide.

Then they started to sing in a language which seemed just as ancient as the earth itself. They play off each other's notes. Andromeda's light ones and Clete's deep ones.

My life had taken a strange course over the past few weeks.

And I originally thought I would have been dead by now.

***

The jolt of the horse woke me.

This was our second night. All around us was now covered in greenery. Be it leaf or moss. It was hard to find patches of brown in the ground or the trees. Andromeda tells me this is one of the few temperate rainforests in the world, and their army uses the cover well.

Eventually, some earthy tones ahead revealed we'd reached our destination.

We entered a circling of homes built of stone and wood. Some of the homes were inside of the trees themselves. Tents were at the center.

I spied a few women looking at us from their homes. They fit in the fashion of the other two warriors. Even their eyes spoke of their unity while presenting temporary curiosity towards Naomi and me.

We all got off the horses and enter a wooded house. A long table awaited us full off colorful food. I recognized the blueberries, blackberries, and strawberries. But there were also cranberries, elderberries, and salmon berries which I was seeing for the first time. The fruit surrounded rows of fresh salmon.

So plump and sweet were those fruits and fish. I teared a little. I'd never had anything this good. This was what food from outside was like? I hadn't had any in my life. Even the Jackal's food was made under controlled circumstances at the base. My parents couldn't afford outside food. And many people who lived in cities were paranoid of outside food. Even with its abundance and proven benefits. People still feared it was toxic. Yet these same people filled themselves with prosthetics and drugs. They wanted to remain in control and they felt letting nature inside would take some that away. Conroy was the same. We weren't allowed to eat outside food either. Only rations he considered chemically pure.

I felt as if my insides were getting oxygen for the first time. My body wanted this food in a way it's never desired anything else.

Andromeda and Clete eagerly ate their fill. Naomi ate with little bites.

I managed to stuff myself with the last of the blueberries before Andromeda spoke.

"You and Naomi will be sharing quarters. I trust you can supervise her?" The question was aimed at Naomi.

"Yes." Naomi said.

"Good. Most of your responsibilities are on Sky of course. But we expect you to aid in the serious illnesses and wounds of our women as needed."

"Of course."

Then Andromeda moved on to me.

She tells me I'd find a role among them. In the meantime, I'd train with them. The idea was training in the wilderness not only prepares you for issues in the natural world, but also the technological one. However, they did have places to train elsewhere closer to these concrete jungles. While I'd train with them, I was considered too young for combat, so I wouldn't be fighting alongside them for years. I wasn't sure if I was relieved or angered by this.

If I escaped as planned, it wouldn't matter anyway.

Though I felt in a strange way, I would be letting down Naomi if I ran off. She didn't seem herself and I couldn't figure out why. Perhaps she was feeling off in a different environment and away from Wild Dog. I didn't want to make it worse.

Naomi and I were led to a hut. I could hear the rumbling of a storm on the horizon. It wouldn't be wise to leave tonight anyway. I needed time to plan.

Inside were two full beds, which surprised me. I think I expected leaves instead of water proof modified cotton. There was a wooden desk and chair. Chemical lights in the ceiling mimicked the constellations we'd seen overhead on the way here.

It gave me a strong urge to paint. I felt a sadness well up in me. I didn't think I was going to be able to paint here. There was no blank concrete canvas in the jungle.

Everything was already covered in some kind of life and story.

Once we were alone, Naomi and I settled in without saying a word to each other.

The storm came. Heavy rain and thunder. Yet the hut held without so much as a shudder. These buildings were constructed with greater technology, even if it didn't seem so from the outside looking in.

Chapter Twenty-Six

It reminded me of another storm. I'd painted Anemoi and Iris on a wall as storm clouds closed in around me. One was the goddess of wind and the other the goddess of rainbows. Anemoi came to me easily. I knew she dried in time for the incoming rain. Iris was harder. I wasn't sure how to envision her, how I was going to get her to appear on the concrete. The rumbling clouds pushed me to make a decision. I didn't think I would have time to finish Iris as the storm approached. I could already feel some drops fall upon me as I wrapped up. Lighting hit right near me, and I was forced to leave the area. I didn't think Iris would make it.

Yet when I returned days later, somehow even her rainbow was still shining through. She looked pristine as if I'd painted her on a sunny day.

A flash of light brought my mind back into the hut. Naomi appeared to be asleep. I wanted to reach out to her in some way, but I didn't know how.

Dreams took me again.

***

I dreamt I was running through the woods. Each time my foot landed, everything became more painful. A man was searching for me, but I couldn't tell if it's Indigo or Aziel. I cried because I wanted to scream but couldn't.

I kept running, not sure if it was safe to turn around. Safe to return to the voice calling my name.

***

"Sky."

Naomi awakened me to golden beams of light coming through the windows.

"Hey." I closed my eyes again for a bit before committing to opening them for the day.

"Here."

She presented a plate of salmon and blueberries to me.

"Thanks."

Clete arrived and escorted me out of the hut. Naomi didn't follow.

Once we reached an area of wood with a small clearing, she handed me a long weapon I'd never seen before. The wood felt off in my fingers. Like this was some kind of technology I wasn't supposed to possess. Its origins went too far back in time from a culture I didn't belong to.

Then I realized it was just a stick. I was being philosophical over a simple stick.

"That's it? That's all I'm training with?"

"Many weapons require similar movement. And you can still do a lot of damage with a staff. You'll learn on your feet quickly. You'll have to."

She wacked my head and swept the staff at my legs so I fell to the earth.

She'd made her point.

I got myself back on my feet.

"Old fashioned weapons can't be hijacked, and they're often unexpected, since most forces only train to deal with the most modern of weapons. Even something like this staff still hold the key in our warfare victories. We still needed to modernize how tactics too or we'd be wiped out. But we still start everyone with the basics."

She used her staff to point to the foliage all around us.

"We also use the land to our advantage. The land and climate itself is still just as important in warfare as it always has been. You'll need to learn how to make it your ally as well."

"And the weather?"

She nodded. "Even a storm can be used to your advantage when one understands the powers of the natural forces which surround us al."

Until evening, Clete worked to teach me blocking techniques and a few attack moves with the staff. Hitting my fingers and other parts when my posture or movement wasn't quite right. But offering a strong nod when she was pleased.

I ate alone with Naomi that night in the hut.

My dreams were haunted by Aziel calling my name.

That was my life for the next two weeks.

***

At the end of those two weeks, Clete lead me to the center of their village. There I was thrown to a group of women with better coordination than a pack of wolves. I only had the staff, feeling more like a stick again, to defend myself.

They didn't hold back as I ended up thrown to the ground or assaulted with their weapons. I was quick to learn to block, dodge, and deflect to avoid the pain; just as I had with Clete.

I went to bed sore without wanting to eat. Naomi still hadn't said much to me since we got here. She hadn't seemed to perform any tests on me either. I was sleeping in fast forward. My dreams were being processed so fast I couldn't seem to remember them well. A mesh of people from my past and present. Looking at my uncertain future.

Then I'm awoke to endure a world of pain once again. I lost count of the days.

***

Soon each time I was in the ring, I felt my speed increasing. The strength in my body starting to flow into the staff like it was second nature. Like I'd been doing this my whole life. The women I was with seemed to be pleased with my progress as well. Clete was more often giving her nod of approval.

I've been fighting for survival my whole life. But I'd never fought in so physical a way. This was the most literal I'd ever been with fighting. I was mentally flashing through old battles of mine as well. Refighting and gaining ground in wars I thought were already won.

There's a whole other mode you get into when you fight. Your mind runs on adrenaline. There's a thrill to it. But also, a focus, as long as you didn't let emotion take over. Pain was placed into a different folder of your mind, to be accessed later as long as it wasn't stopping you completely.

There's tunnel vision between you and your opponents. Your movements come so naturally and so quickly, that it's as if you're not even in control of them at all. But it's you. All you. Those were the choices you're making. Missing a block so you received a blow to the stomach. The dive which missed the kick just in time. That flying fist knocked your rival out cold.

It wasn't the same kind of high I got while painting. It was totally new.

Especially when these warriors invited me to their table to eat.

***

Though one day I went too far. A brutality released from me. A girl who continually tripped me in the past did so once again and I finally snapped. She had been the most unforgiving in her attacks besides Clete. I didn't want her taking advantage of my lack of skill any longer. I refused to be weak as I had in the past. By my parents. By my gang.

I tricked her into thinking I was going for her head and went for her legs instead. She fell over like a large tree.

I jumped on her and screamed. I pounded with my fists on her until blood pooled out from several wells of her face, eagerly being drunk by the earth. I was tackled from behind.

"This is not how you're to treat a comrade." Clete hissed.

"After you all beat me? Isn't that what you're looking to do? Turn me into a killing machine?" I stood to face her. Then I charged at her.

Clete flipped me over, my face was to the sky and my back was to the dirt.

"That's not the intention. It's to avoid fighting at all costs. Know that it's there so that things may be resolved in another way. Only fight when it's absolutely necessary. Fight to the level the situation calls for. Only aim to kill when no other choice is granted."

"I don't understand the connection."

"You'll need to."

She lowered her hand and raised me back up.

"Never give up your own life easily. Fighting to stay alive is critical. Turning to anger in a fight will cost you your life. You'll need to channel your emotions in another way."

"Then why not tell me all of this before?"

"You need to know where you're starting with for yourself as a fighter before you can find your way as a true warrior."

"What about your wars then?"

"We only fight when absolutely necessary. Though there are times when that's more often than any of us would want."

Chapter Twenty-Seven

What was worth dying for? Most of the women agreed a comrade was worth dying for. All of them agreed their leader, Andromeda, was worth laying their life for. There was no question in that. Those are the things I heard while eating with those warriors.

I apologized to the woman I beat up. She said she'd done the same to another a long time ago. She mentioned Clete had told her the same thing a long time ago, her anger wasn't worth dying for.

Sharing the hut with Naomi that night, I asked what she thought was worth dying for. Considering her history, her first answer wasn't surprising.

"Life."

Her second was.

"And love."

"Love?" I responded.

She nodded.

"Even if the feeling isn't mutual."

"I wasn't expecting you to say that."

"Why?"

"Love doesn't seem to play a critical role in your life."

"It does."

Chapter Twenty-Eight

I awoke in a cold sweat. I didn't remember what I dreamed of.

I felt like I'd lost something and was unsure how to get it back. Or if it could ever be mine again. Perhaps it was something I never had in the first place.

Was it the Chip? Did it really disturb me so much that it was gone? That it was completely out of me? It's not like the thing belonged in my body in the first place. It was about to kill me. That thing wasn't beneficial to me. If I was lucky, there would be no permanent damage.

Yet it ignited a power I never felt in my life, but never got the chance to use before I understood it. Before it was taken away. It led me to a connection with another human being which went beyond sexual or romantic drives. Even with those still being factors, the alterations from the chip, surviving it, and its power were the main lines of connection. Leading to a communication which went beyond language. Which went beyond emotion or thought.

Now that it was gone, I felt like I didn't know who I was anymore. What I was supposed to do.

Why had Aziel made his way to me? What drew him to do this to me in the first place? Did he already know I was the right candidate? Or did it not matter, and it just took someone to survive the chip. Perhaps I was the first to survive besides him.

Why had it changed things between us so much? And what did it mean now that it was gone? How much more was going to change?

I still wasn't sure if he had a chip himself. Especially if his could have killed him as well.

What secrets was he hiding from me? What secrets were hidden from myself?

There might not be anything left in me. That's what I should had hoped for. That I could go back to being a normal human being. That I wouldn't forever be a bioweapon or altered by technology I didn't understand.

Naomi had started testing on me again but didn't have any more answers for me.

***

My eyes opened to blue light. The whole hut was illuminated. I looked around for the source, until I realized it was me. My whole body radiated blue neon light.

I felt a charge growing with me. The familiar electrical energy. It was stronger now. Was Aziel nearby? I was suddenly a live wire, a lighting storm. But I knew Aziel was nowhere in sight. This was me.

My energy was going crazy in a different way. It wasn't moving in the ways I was expecting. My whole body was electric. Not just a few parts. I could explode into a lightning storm at any moment.

What was I going to do?

"Sky!"

Naomi was awake now. Getting instruments ready.

"Don't touch me!" I screamed.

"I'm here to help you!"

"I'm not going to let this hurt you again."

Or anyone else.

I ran out of the hut and into the forest. I could hear Naomi calling for the others to help her. Calling me to stop. But I couldn't. I was so scared of what this charge was going to do.

I ran until my lungs were on fire and needed the strength of a large tree to hold me up. They'd find me unless I kept going. I couldn't let it happen.

Suddenly a new thought came to me.

Shut it off yourself.

I breathed more slowly now. I raised my hands to the sky and released a shock into space. Night turned into surreal bluish daylight for a moment before turning back into darkness. I closed my eyes. Then I imagined I was collecting all the remaining electric energy in my body back into my center. When I opened my eyes, the blue glow was gone.

Exhaustion overcame me. I fell to the ground.

Naomi found me shortly after. Followed by Andromeda.

"Why did you run?"

"I was scared I was going to kill you all." I still was struggling to catch my breath.

Naomi checked my pulse and examined me.

"The glow and charge are gone."

"Something in my head told me I could stop it myself. And I did."

"The chip has proven to have permanently changed your body. I suspected this was the case based on the last few tests. Your old currents were slowly reemerging, even if you didn't feel them. But you can learn to control it. This is who you are now."

"Goddess must have intervened to help you." Andromeda said, "This is a special tree you found. Look on the other side."

I followed Andromeda's eyes with my own as well. The tree was huge, branches and leaves curling high into the night sky, seeming to touch the moon and stars themselves. The trunk would take a whole circle of warriors to get around. As I walked closer I saw its roots weren't buried in earth but exposed in the air. The tree was holding itself in the air by its roots into the sides of a cliff.

Below the cliff was a beach which ran into the ocean, and then the sky.

"This is our tree of life. Many of our warriors have come here looking for guidance and aid. You found it without even knowing where it was. Goddess led you here. Perhaps she'll let you know in time if she hasn't revealed herself to you already."

Andromeda drew her sword and aimed it to the stars. She kneeled and thanked whoever assisted in keeping me safe and guiding my way.

"In time present yourself to our warrior so she may fully serve you."

She then spoke in the ancient language she spoke with Clete.

Chapter Twenty-Nine

It was still late when Naomi and I returned to our cabin. I expected Naomi to want to run a ton of tests. But for now, she seemed as content as I to crawl into bed and fall asleep.

In the morning she told me I'd need to skip training for the day, so she could check for a few things. After charging her equipment in the sun, she returned to the privacy of our hut.

She asked me to charge myself fully. She then wanted me to draw electricity into isolated body parts. I managed to do so. Though the first time a shock shot out from my arm into the ground. But soon I was able to draw current into my fingers and toes, my lips and eyes, while keeping it in control. She asked me to glow again. I managed all the colors, even a rainbow all at once. She even asked me to attempt to charge a dead battery. She placed it in my hand and I sent charge into it. I succeeded when she placed the battery into an old-fashioned flashlight and it turned on. She checked me with all her gadgets, though I wasn't sure what she was finding despite her slight smile. Just when Naomi was putting away her equipment and I thought she was done, she asked me for one more thing.

"Do one more thing for me."

"What?"

"Touch me with the current."

"What?"

"I want you to send some of the current into my body."

"I almost killed you last time! That's exactly why I ran off last night."

"Based on my tests, I'll survive even if something goes wrong."

"Naomi!"

"I trust you. You can do this."

She offered me her hand. I hesitated for a moment. There was a seriousness in her eyes which told me not to turn her down.

I grabbed her hand and she closed her eyes. After a deep breath, I sent as little current into her as I could. I saw her smile.

"Send more. It's ok."

I did.

The look on Naomi's face was one of euphoria. It was as if she was flying. I'd never seen her look so free.

I sent in more current in turn. Blue light shined within and around us. We continued to ride with each other higher until I was ready to let go.

Naomi kept her eyes closed for another few moments until her gaze met mine.

"You gave me a lot to work with."

"How did it feel for you?"

"As if the whole universe was coursing through my veins. Though it didn't feel it in the same way I suspect it feels for you. I could feel the current ending in me while it continued to circle in you. We all contain certain mysteries that, as hard as we try, we can never share it fully with others. This is yours to own and foster."

Naomi brushed her hair out of her face.

"You can go now if you want." Naomi was packing her equipment back into her suitcase.

I went to leave the hut to see if there was still time to train. As I left I heard Naomi speak to me once more.

"Thank you, Sky."

***

When I returned to the hut that night, I saw a cream colored horse waiting near the entrance. I went to pet it on the snout. As I did so, I saw Indigo speaking to Naomi in our doorway. My heart raced even before his eyes met mine. I entered the hut.

"What are you doing here?" I asked Indigo.

"I'm here for a report on you." He said.

"Wild Dog was ok with sending you?"

"What does that mean?"

"Never mind."

I didn't know what else to say to him.

Naomi excused herself to recharge her solar equipment and left us alone. I sat on my bed and he sat at the desk. We faced each other to speak.

"So, what do you need from me?"

"I got the basics on the chip from Naomi. But how are you holding up here?"

"Well despite getting my ass kicked on a regular basis, I'm actually beginning to like it."

"Really?"

"Yeah."

"You have some bruising, so I was concerned."

It was true. Black, blue, and brown spots speckled me like a Leopard on my arms and legs. They didn't hurt as bad as they did before. They seemed to be healing faster than before too.

"You have put on some weight. In a good way. I know girls don't like hearing that."

"I'm happy about it. I'm not so scrawny. I've been eating well here."

"A happy stomach builds morale."

"I can see that."

We sat there silently for a while. There was so much more I wanted to say to him. I knew it was the same for him.

Naomi returned. We all spoke until the night returned and deepened. Mostly about the differences between the two armies. There was a lot more joking than I expected from either of them.

"How is Wild Dog?" Naomi finally asked what I knew she wanted to all along.

"Actually, I should have told you sooner. That's also why I'm here."

Naomi's eyes shifted to fear.

"He's alive." Indigo quickly added, "But he needs you. He's had some strange symptoms that we can't figure out. He can't hide it from the men much longer."

"What kind of symptoms?"

"Could I have caused this?" I asked.

"No. It's related to the plate in his brain." Indigo said.

"What are his symptoms?" Naomi repeated.

"Mostly been extreme headaches and shakes. Some minor hallucinations as well. He's still acting like himself. Most of the men don't even know. He's been hiding it well."

"Any chance we can leave tonight?"

"If you feel it best. Then yes."

"We need to."

Naomi went to pack the rest of her few belongings.

"She'll be fine here. She has a handle on herself." Naomi assured Indigo.

"You need to stay here, Sky." Indigo said.

"Alone. With these women?"

"You said yourself you like it here."

"Yeah but Naomi has been…"

I hadn't realized until that moment how much I'd been emotionally depending on Naomi's presence for a sense of security and comfort. How it scared me to be losing her. But I refused to cry. I wasn't going to guilt Indigo or Naomi. Not in those circumstances. Not while

Wild Dog's life may be on the line. I could handle this. I needed to.

Before leaving Naomi turned to me.

"Sky, you don't need me anymore. I'm so proud of how you've handled all of this."

"You don't think I'm a danger anymore?"

"No. Not with the spirit you have. I trusted you with my life, and you proved yourself worthy of the responsibility bestowed upon you."

She left the hut.

Indigo turned to me.

"The moment I can return I will."

"You will?"

"I need to know you're alright here. Duty or not."

I felt a strong urge to kiss him right then and there. But I didn't.

He seemed to move towards me for a moment before stopping himself.

"I'll see you soon. I promise."

With that he left the hut. I watched Indigo and Naomi ride off into the night.

Chapter Thirty

Indigo.

While my feelings towards him were complicated, they were also strong. Perhaps they weren't so complicated. Perhaps I was making it this way. Or he was too. Perhaps we were both running away from our feelings, letting circumstance be an easy out. Or even our other emotional baggage.

I used to let my imagination flow with his as he told me of the life we could build together. Of what we could have, of what our future would look like. I was there dreaming right alongside him as we stared into the clouds. At night, it would be the stars.

But when I wasn't with him, my thoughts turned elsewhere. So much in my life was telling me those things we dreamed were impossible. How could anyone love me really? My own parents resented me. No one else seemed to hold any real love for me. I felt in time Indigo would resent me too. He'd blame me when the dreams didn't come together. Or find a prettier and better girl who fit into his fantasy even better.

I was a mess. A horrible awful mess. With nothing to give him. Nothing to share. And I refused to take anything away from him. Which is why I left without telling him. His life would be better without me. Those dreams would be closer in reach with me out of the way. Perhaps one day he would even be happy I wasn't there at all. That's what I told myself.

Perhaps I'd see him living his dream as I watched from the distance. Saw him with his beautiful girl in his beautiful life. Whether it was out in the woods. Or the new condos which balanced modern and natural life. I'd smile knowing he achieved everything he deserved.

I could live amongst the slime and scum I belonged with. The only life I was ever good for. The only life which would accept me. It wasn't a dream, and I wasn't a dream. So, I couldn't ruin any of it.

Even with my gang, my art, becoming Conroy's lover, my situation with Aziel, the chip, I never forgot Indigo. I tried to. I even tried a memory erasing machine Conroy let me borrow. But it seemed to only intensify the memories further. Showing me how real all my feelings were, despite the choices I'd made.

What were my feelings really? I didn't understand them. But I missed him. That I knew. Even if my reasoning was intangible.

***

Aziel haunted my dreams in the night. He was on top of me, pinning me to the concrete below. I scrambled to get away. No matter how hard I tried I couldn't escape. An electric cord between us kept me tethered to him. The cord was sending more and more currents through me, and despite my struggle I felt I was becoming more his with each moment. Even though I didn't want to be.

Chapter Thirty-One

That morning, Clete handed me a wooden sword.

"Is this really an improvement from my stick?" I asked.

"A broad sword has similar movements to a staff. It will prepare you for the real thing. Better to use wood before you face the realities fighting with steel."

It was hard for me to believe. But she'd proven to be right over and over again.

Clete picked up her own wooden sword.

As we worked on technique all through the morning and until dusk, I saw Clete was correct. Both weapons shared similarities in striking and blocking. Unlike the staff, the sword allowed me to leave my other hand free if I wished. Allowing me to deflect certain attacks and flexibility in movement with the weapon I didn't have while grasping it with both hands.

Though the sword, even a wooden one, held itself with a type of grace; especially when it was being used. Watching it cut through the air, reminded me of how an ice skate would glide across the ice. The mark of the sword was still apparent even if it didn't land its target.

I felt like I was learning how to paint in the air. Our work was called Martial Arts for a reason. It was an art reproduced with practice and use. But it was even more temporary than my painting. A flash in the air and the movement transformed into something else. A block turned into a take down. A kick took a higher route. A punch found a new target. The weapon changed course with incredibly speed. Each movement had a meaning all its own which created a larger scene all together. A story was told whether one fought alone, with another, or amongst many. This reminded me of bringing individual colors of the paints into shapes, which turned into larger images and snapshots of scenes. Everyone still had a meaning and purpose all its own, but together it created something so much larger.

Combat had meaning.

Even war.

***

My loneliness didn't set in until I returned to the hut. I was the only one to occupy it that night.

Andromeda, Clete, and the others were aware of Naomi's departure. Yet they didn't send anyone else to me. Perhaps they were starting to trust me. Or didn't view my privacy as a threat.

Clearly, I wasn't one of them at the moment, but they weren't trying to make me feel like an outsider, or a criminal, or a bioweapon. Instead they were taking the time to train me. Increase my skill. They were actually making me more dangerous. They didn't feel threatened by me. They saw some value in making me better instead. But why? What did they see in me? What did they want from me? Perhaps I was just another body available for training and it was simple as that. They just needed more fighters for war and would use my abilities in time for their own victories.

I was still figuring them out myself.

I didn't talk to any of them much besides what little I needed to say. This was partly out of fear. These were powerful women who knew how to fight. Some of them had a high level of intelligence and wit to go with it. Mostly it was because their world was still so alien to me. The fact they believed so strongly in things I wanted to think were real, but logically grappled with. Their focus was on combat training as well as the outside world. Their natural feel of the weather, the seasons, the earth itself. They didn't run away from the feel of dirt or a spotted berry, they embraced it. Yet they were so clean compared to the people I'd known in the city; even the rich ones I'd seen. There was an earthy smell these women carried, each with their individual signature. Smoke and tea. Earth and herb. Wood and berry. Flower and Metal.

I wondered if my own smell had changed at all. I wasn't sure what my smell was before. If the paint ever sunk into my skin and became part of me. Or the concrete and technology which surrounded me.

Or the chip.

Chapter Thirty-Two

I'd left the door open this night, a move I would have never made in the city since it would have cost me my life. Even in the wilderness it was a huge risk. Yet leaving the door open made Naomi's absence less painful. I felt closer to the tribe of warrior women surrounding me and the creatures outside.

Just as I was falling asleep I heard wolves howling. Then one of our warrior women howled back in turn. I arose and followed the sounds.

A woman who I'd seen often but never spoken too stood next to the woods. Her long curly brown hair blended with trees themselves. Her pale skin was speckled like a pebbled stream. Tonight, she wasn't wearing anything at all, and seemed to glow under the full moon.

From a distance, I watched as she called to the wolves and they called back. I couldn't see the wolves, they remained invisible in the density of the trees. But I felt them.

She turned around.

"Want to try it?" She asked.

I was startled.

"I wouldn't know how." I replied.

"Yes, you do." She beckoned me over.

She called to the wolves once more and they called back in turn.

"Now make an 'o' shape with your mouth and open your throat. Go as loud as you can."

A sound emerged from me I didn't know I was capable of. I sounded just like her, just like one of the wolves. The vibration and sound let me express all my loneliness, everything else I'd ever felt in my life. It echoed into the trees and mountains.

I heard one call in turn. Though I would never know the wolf's story word for word, I could feel the truth of their story reach into my soul and body.

I used my currents to see if I could feel him and the others more deeply. I felt all fourteen of them. The one calling to me I had the strongest feel for, but with the others I could still feel a sense of who they were; their emotions and stories. All this without even seeing them. Without making eye contact. Without knowing their language.

The woman and I kept calling into the night and the wolves kept calling back.

**

There was something beautiful about the first sight upon waking being the trees. The air flowed into me and the sight breathed something into me. Inspiration? Life? Spirit?

Next to me was the woman who called to the wolves with me the night before. She was just rousing from sleep.

At least for the moment, I didn't feel so lonely anymore.

"Do you remember me?" she asked. Her green eyes were wide open now.

"I don't."

"I remember you."

"How do you know me?"

"My name had been Spark in my old life due to how well I worked with electronics and explosives. I am now Wolf. Andromeda gave me that name when she found me calling to wolves as you did last night."

I finally realized, she was from my old gang. Sparkle looked different back then. Her eyes weren't nearly as bright and looked browner than the green I saw now. Her hair had been short and neon green. She had a long clear prosthetic sleeve over her arm. I looked and saw it was now all skin covered by a knotted tattoo of wolves. She had been under weight like me but gained muscle since. She looked beautiful now in a way I never thought she could. If she never said anything, I don't think I would have ever figured out where she'd come from. I would have assumed she was born into this warrior woman life.

She was long gone before the chip was put in me though. Someone from the gang had been hired to kill her for refusing a job which would have killed many people. She ended up killing them and escaping instead.

She'd been considered weak among my gang. It was assumed she had OD'd or something along those lines, even when her assassinator was found dead. I'd suspected something more but questioning anything like that could get you killed. And since her and I were never close, she was always elsewhere on a job, I didn't push it.

She heard of Infinity through rumors which were whispered amongst those living on the streets. They were looking for recruits. They were offering a much better life to women who wanted to join. Truthfully for many, such as her, good food was more than enough of an enticement.

The screening process was particularly grueling. The first day of training made most quit. But not her. She wanted out. She would do anything to never need to return to our gang ever again. Anything to get rid of the prosthetic skin. Any way to have a chance at her own life.

Infinity trained her in secret. Wolf kept her double life a secret from our gang. Finally, she was able to kill the man who attempted to kill her. Then she ran back to the women. Far into the woods on an empty belly. She'd passed out along the way. Infinity found her there lying amongst the leaves and twigs. They saved her from the infection from the prosthetic skin. With herbs and medicines, the best of ancient tradition and modern science, unavailable to those in the gang, she was healed. They removed it slowly over time and her real skin grew back.

When Wolf finished her story, I felt a sense of remorse for not having to get to know her sooner. Perhaps both of our lives would have been much better. Perhaps I could have left with her.

Or perhaps it's better that we were learning of each other now. Now that we were both striped of our old layers which were only there to protect us. Now we could be true to who we are to each other.

"I've always loved your painting."

"Thank you."

"I would like it if you could work with me. I need a partner for our tattoos and weapon designs. You'd be perfect for the job."

"I didn't realize you were an artist as well."

"I kept it secret until I came here. I didn't feel safe to express myself until then. You've always been so brave and bold in your work. I haven't met anyone else here that I feel could handle my workshop like you can."

I felt a sense of guilt having not remembered her before. But the prospect before me was too good to pass up.

"I'd love that. I've been itching to paint for so long. I haven't been able to since Wild Dog and his men picked me up."

"Great. I'll need to ask Andromeda for approval, but she rarely says no to anyone over things like this. But once she's says yes, I'll get you set up with me."

With that she ran off toward her hut.

I headed back to the clearing for the day's combat training.

Chapter Thirty-Three

The air in my lungs seemed to empower and drive me. Even as I continued to get my ass kicked. The earth was there to support me as I fought and gave me the extra motivation not to fall. The trees gave me cover and places to hide. The sky, my sky, our sky, binding us. The sky let me dream and believe in those dreams fully without hesitation for the first time.

Those women seemed inspired in their training as well. These women wanted to make me stronger. Make each other stronger as well as their individual selves. They see my strength as their strength. As all of our strength together as a whole fighting force.

We took a break to watch the highest trained fighters go at it. Their weapons were individualistic. They fit the personalities and inner soul of each fighter. The choices in wood, be it white oak or bamboo. Choices in metals, be it traditional steel or the newly refined color changing one. How those materials were used; making sais, swords, or staff. The colors and designs. Casings meant to honor the dead: a beloved pet or a departed tree.

Clete seemed to enjoy herself immensely as four women ran at her and she threw them to the ground single handedly.

I was currently only using practice pieces of course. But I was truly looking forward to having weapons of my own. Weapons which were truly an extension of me. Weapons which went beyond being simple warfare tools.

***

Between training sessions, I was finally able to observe the women more closely.

They had these beautiful large communal bath houses. Taking hot mud baths and spring water baths was amazing. Some days, I spent hours in the evening simply going back and forth between them while enjoying the sensations.

I didn't mind being naked in front of these women. There's no sense they'll judge me or take advantage of me.

They often walked around with barely any clothes at all. It was extra motivation to ensure they would avoid getting hit in practice combat. It better prepared them for the real thing.

It was now the same for me. I wore enough to feel at least somewhat modest, even if it wouldn't be considered anywhere near that in my street life. I was so much more open to showing my body than I ever had.

I'd feared women for years. Feeling they aren't really on your side. Feeling a man could be better at least, even if they were likely to drop you when they found their new toy. While women would take revenge on you. Hurt you. Make you suffer.

Each of our unique talents builds up this greater whole. In my gang life individuality was often squash. It was always about the mission. Always about the goal of the leader. Yes, the goals and purpose are important. But we, as individuals also matter. Our individual missions. Our individual selves. Even how our opinions differed on important topics matter. It helps us evolve into a greater whole and ever greater purpose. We all had our purpose. We all were driving each other forward as we drove ourselves forward.

They were the perfect combination of using nature in warfare and understanding technologies role in combat.

Their religion is an ancient pagan one. A group of Druids from Ireland were exiled to Greece for a time until they were able to return; coming back with a belief in both Celtic and Greek deities. This was the ancestry and traditions of Andromeda and many of their other women. They believed in the Goddesses I longed to be real.

They kept their hair long and free, which I hadn't really seen too many women do in my own life. Even Naomi kept hers in a tight bun.

Women of Infinity avoided getting any technological implants. And used medical drugs sparingly. They have all these weird natural remedies that seem to magically work somehow.

Chapter Thirty-Four

Wolf approached me a few evenings later to inform me Andromeda approved of my apprenticeship with her. She said I could start with her in the next few days after she had prepped some starting materials for me.

In the meantime, she told me to check out the tattoos the women had while sketching out my own. She even gave me a notebook and pencils to work with.

Most of the women had tattoos of animals, Goddesses, or knots. Some had all three. They're used for identification as well as personality. As well as to inspire certain fighting qualities. Like fox qualities. Or lion qualities.

At night I let my hand fly over the pages, watching the stories unravel before me. Stories of owls and wolves. Of ancient tradition. Or the Goddesses. I would flash right back to my street art. The urge to paint was being fulfilled, even if it was in another way.

Perhaps I could stay out here for the rest of my life. Especially now that I had my art back.

***

That night I dreamed of Aziel again. He and Conroy were in a sword match. Conroy was swinging wildly and Aziel smiled as he easily dodged each blow. He killed Conroy with one cut, beheading him. Then Aziel approached to try to take me again. Except this time, I was ready. I had my sword. Blow after blow I blocked, as did he with him. Exhaustion threatened to overtake me. Then I remembered the cord between us and realized I could use it to my advantage. But before I had the chance to defeat him, I woke up.

***

I met Wolf in her workshop. The wood walls were decorated with sketches of knots work and woodland predators. Some were colored in. The smell of sage, ink, and cedar filled the space. Tables aligned the walls with colored inks and books full of designs. At the center was a table to lay on and a table topped with equipment to design the skin. There was a retractable wooden chair on the other side of the room. The far-right corner had a mirror facing the entrance.

Wolf told me we would also be aiding with the designs for weapons and other things. Though tattooing was what I was most excited about.

Wolf showed me an ink which was designed to be invisible in the daylight, but fully illuminate in the darkness depending on the adrenal rate of the bearer. The idea was to scare enemies in battle. Old fashioned ink which could be seen in daylight in order to express themselves and strike fear into their enemies. Inks which changed color based on the emotions running beneath it, good to transition from battle to regular life.

Wolf stressed all the inks were difficult to remove once it was in the skin. But the new inks were nearly impossible. So, it made it vital to get the designs right the first time. This intimidated me. With my street art, I knew I could at least paint over something if I messed up. The newer inks weren't so forgiving in that department. The cells of the skin changed after the first ink was added and would destroy other colors which were added.

Wolf told me the first few weeks of my apprenticeship I would be cleaning equipment and watching her work. I'd be able to move on to practicing on fruit skin after that. I was glad, even though I was excited I didn't want everything handed to me either. I liked the idea of having to work at it.

I watched her etch fairy wings into a woman's back. Giving her the ability to fly in a symbolic way. I watched with interest. Sure, I loved my concrete canvas, but having a walking and living human canvas? The idea drove me wild.

But it also terrified me. Forever marking another human being? Changing them forever with my own hand? My hand retraced to the scar on my stomach.

Though Wolf told me it could be a while until I was ready to ink designs onto human skin.

And it was.

2123

Chapter Thirty-Five

A year and a half went by. I'd train certain days and aid in Wolf's workshop other days. In that time, I earned my own sword. Clete presented it to me herself. The metal was sky blue and the handle jet black. It had been designed for me in secret. I was honored to receive such a gift.

I'd painted some murals in a few of the women's homes, presenting tales of the forest and the religion they held so dear. The paints provided were a mixture of berries and other sources which allowed the art to be natural but lasting. I was even commissioned to repaint the bathhouse. There I created a mural of the goddess Eireen in the water with her dolphins.

My own hut had been repainted to my liking as well. I turned it into an enchanted forest full of trees with sparkling leaves and animals which transformed into the Goddesses themselves.

I continued to practice tattooing on fruit in between tending to Wolf's workshop.

I didn't use the powers from the chip too much. I was too busy most of the time to think about it. But occasionally I'd try a new trick, like brightening the constellations in my hut's ceiling or seeing if I could send a charge into the stars themselves.

I'd wonder about Indigo during the day, and the army he was part of.

Aziel haunted me at night.

***

The day came Wolf told me it was time for me to tattoo someone for real. She asked me to sketch based on what a woman named Xena was commissioning. She wanted Athena and her owl. I drew a few images over the course of several days and showed them to Xena. Wolf informed me of the one Xena picked one.

Then the day came when it was time for me to imprint the art itself. Wolf told me I was ready.

I didn't feel ready. I shook all that morning before the appointment. I wanted this so bad. But it was so unlike what I've done before. This was a living breathing human being who I was messing with. I thought of the prosthetic skins, the see-through body parts, and even the chip which had been inside me. How was this any different?

The girl who showed up was blond. While she'd seen my sketches through Wolf, this was the first time we were face to face in the workshop. Xena reminded me of the girls you'd imagine would be running around the fields picking flowers. But she was far from naive and innocent. You could see her age and experience in her eyes, which showed she was involved with the same world as all of us.

Xena didn't even look at Wolf. She looked at me and ensured I understood where she wanted the artwork.

She took off her top and laid herself across the table. Her back was a pure white canvas. I touched her skin with my bare hand, just like I would do with a wall before I started. This would be her first tattoo.

I was so scared of ruining her beautiful skin. Every wrong move would be staring back at me and the rest of the world. Whether I made good art or bad, I'd be hurting her in the process. I didn't have to worry about that with a wall. But I guess a wall wasn't ever experiencing my art fully. Not like a person would.

I let my hand continue to glide over her back. I used the power from the chip to feel her more deeply. I'd never used it for my art before. I felt her life come back to meet mine. This was so much more dynamic than concrete. This was a real life connecting and responding to mine. I could see in her mind what she wanted for herself. I felt her full trust in me.

I was ready for the ink and needles.

Once I was into it though, it was just like my spray paints. I got so wrapped up into the creative world of what I was doing that everything just flowed into a beautiful work of art. This was my world for the time being. Colors met each other in harmony. The image and scene revealed itself. Just like my street painting.

Then it's finished, and I come back to the rest of the world. I looked up and see Wolf nodding with a grin. The work is done.

I brought Xena to the mirror and gave her another smaller one, so she can see the work. She gasped and then smiled gracefully. I was pleased with my work and so was she. Athena stood powerful and strong with her helmet under her left arm and her owl perched on the other. There was a realism there I'd never seen painting on a wall. After a long while of admiring herself in the mirror, she handed Wolf the small mirror and hugged me with all her might. A wall could never give me a hug like that. Now she'd walk around, always carrying this piece, my piece, with her in pride.

***

Soon everyone wanted my tattoos. One after the other, the women came to allow me to etch my versions of the Goddesses on their bodies. Occasionally animals too, though knot work and animals was more Wolf's specialty so the women tended to want her version. Wolf even tattooed over my old gang mark. Now a Falcon flew there, ready to meet the sky.

I was so happy to be busy doing something creative again. Using my hands on a living moving canvas. Seeing how different pieces looked together on someone's body. A whole life could be told there.

These Goddesses became real to me as the women I inked them on. The trees, seas, and foxes. The wings and faeries. The memorial symbols. They were equally real in this world. Since they were part of the same living breathing canvas. These images would forever live among side them. Whether in the battlefield, mourning a loved one, sleeping under a tree, making love under the stars. These images would be carried with them until they died. Weightless. But forever real.

Chapter Thirty-Six

Six months after I started, Wolf told me I didn't need her constant supervision anymore. I was given my own workspace. It's another wooden circular building at the east edge of the village. I quickly painted the walls in tribute to my favorite mural from my old main hideout. I recreated the forest which transformed into the beach and then the ocean. Except this time, I added the tree of life with its suspended roots and cliff which transition the woodland to the shore.

When I finished, I realized this piece was superior to what I've done before in its depth and detail. Its feeling. The Goddesses faces each held an individuality my old work didn't have. Animals were more realistic now that I'd seen more of them first hand. The scenery took on a life of its own now that I'd interacted with real nature.

This wasn't the art of the angsty girl longing for something else, despite feeling it to be impossible to have. Here I was creating the worlds I wanted. I'd always been doing it, even back in my street art days. But now they were truly taking on a life of their own, whether on a wall or on a person.

My art wasn't just an image of hope, it created new realities while interacting with the one I was living in. One where I didn't feel the constant struggle for survival. Here I was supported by others and able to do something I loved, which also gave something beautiful back to this same community. All the while I surrounded us all with beautiful art.

My twenty-year-old self wouldn't have believed any of this to be possible.

But my twenty-two-year-old self, now knew this to be true.

***

That night I dreamed of Aziel. I stood before him. He tried to take me to the ground, but I flipped him over my shoulder. As a result, I knocked him out cold.

I thought it was over.

Then I felt a pulsing sensation where the chip use to be inside of me. My vision was taken to a place far away, where I saw the chip coming back to life. It was glowing blue and calling to me.

Aziel rose and smiled before disappearing before my eyes.

Electricity burst out of me. I'd lost control of managing the currents within me and felt a pain as if I were burning alive. I fell to the floor.

Even in my dream state, I realized the chip had awakened again.

Chapter Thirty-Seven

My screams woke myself and others in the village. Wolf arrives with some of the others, followed shortly by Clete. I screamed for them to get away, before Clete jerked me back to reality. To my relief, I wasn't exploding in electricity. I remained in control of the currents within me. Though I wasn't sure how much longer it would be the case.

"I need to see Andromeda, right now."

Clete nodded in understanding. "Get dressed first."

It was still dark when I made it to Andromeda's designated hut for important meetings. She was already dressed and alert as well. She rose from the large wooden table as I entered the room. Clete was to her right. No one else was in the room.

I reported the dream to her. She exhaled in response.

"I know that it was a dream but…"

"Naomi had told us you were likely to have dreams which would tell of things which were happening related to the chip. That it might have been our only warning."

"Really? She never told me that."

"She told us this in a message after she left, so you'd find this information out at the right time."

"I could have thought it was just a crazy dream and not told you! She hasn't said a word to me since I last saw her almost two years ago!"

"She said it would be so overwhelming when it happened that there would be no way for you to deny it. She told us what we needed to know so we could best handle you and prepare you when the time came."

I sighed. "Naomi should have told me. I thought she told me everything she knew about the chip. What else did Naomi tell you that I don't know about?"

"That the chip was stolen from the Jackals. That it was likely to be reactivated once it was in a secured location. When it was, you could have moments of control loss with your inner currents."

"What?" Tears were flowing down my cheeks. "Then I'll leave right now if I'm a threat."

Andromeda shook her head.

"This is no time for tears. We've instilled better than that in you. You're a part of our tribe now and we're not going to give up on you so easily. Living in constant fear will or exiling you won't solve the bigger problem that someone has a hold of your old chip and is likely also looking for you. That is the bigger problem for us, and the world at large. We still need you here as part of the resolution."

"Do you know who stole it?"

"One of the men got too close to the chip without the right equipment. The theory is, it controlled his brain causing him to take the chip out of the facility. The men have tracking equipment within them as well, but the chip messed with the server on this man. The Jackals weren't able to find him until his body washed up near our shore and the chip was nowhere to be seen. Whoever, he brought the chip to, likely was also the one who killed him."

"Aziel." I whispered.

"Get some rest. We'll need you to help us find the chip in the morning."

Somehow, I was able to go back to sleep when I arrived home.

***

The next morning, I arrived back to Andromeda's meeting spot. The other women were at the table, already discussing plans which hushed as I entered the room.

"Do you have a sense of where the chip is?" Andromeda asked.

I was quiet as I felt for the chip. Then I nodded.

"There a man-made island forty miles west of us. That is where it is."

"Can you point to it on this map?" Andromeda gestured to the one on the table.

I placed my finder over the spot. Clete clearly marked it in red ink.

"That is all, you're dismissed." Andromeda said.

"You don't need me for anything else?" I asked.

"No. Naomi has given us all the information we need to know. Clete will find you if we need anything else.

I went to training after. I didn't stop shaking for nearly two hours. I couldn't hold my practice weapons and went back to my hut without dinner. I crawled into bed and stayed there until the next morning.

Chapter Thirty-Eight

It rained the next day. I sketched in my book working on a new piece Leo had requested.

Then the smell of sandalwood broke me out of the world I was in, while alerting me to the sounds of dirt shifting and leaves crunching. I turned to see what my heart already knew.

"You're really fit now."

I look down at myself. It was true. I almost had a six pack. My legs and arms were toned. My body was tanned and strengthened under the fighting sun.

"There's still some blue in your hair."

I didn't have access to the injections, so the gene could no longer be activation. Only a few streaks remained.

"What took you so long?" I asked.

"Wild Dog sent me to Africa."

"Why?"

"There was a language feud. People no longer want English to be the dominant language when the native population speaking Afrikaans will soon surpass the English ones."

"So, is it over?"

"No. But there's been a lull in the fighting for now."

"Conveniently, Wild Dog was able to keep you away from me?"

Indigo looked towards my artwork on the table.

"We didn't know if you were trustworthy. It was hard to predict what you were and what you would do."

"We or He?"

Indigo's eyes met mine.

"I didn't hide the fact we had a past very well. Naomi was able to confirm it for sure later based on a conversation you two had."

I felt a punch to the gut. I thought that was a private conversation. But I had just assumed that. It made more sense she would tell Wild Dog everything.

"So, I'm the reason you were sent away?"

"I would have needed to go anyway. But yes, he thought it was best to keep us apart until your loyalties were proven."

"What about now?"

"At this point, you've proven yourself. Wild Dog doesn't see you as a threat anymore."

"How?"

"Between Naomi's words and the praises of the women's army, he feels that's more than enough to present your character."

At least Naomi's breach of privacy also proved to my benefit.

"I was never on my gang's side in the first place."

"Was that really the case all along?"

"Did you really think I belonged to those type of people?"

"I told you that you didn't."

"Exactly. And I'm never going back to that."

He smiled. "Good."

"You're not concerned about me being a bioweapon though?"

"Naomi said the loss of control on your end due to someone else acquiring and activating your old chip is becoming less likely. She needed to be honest about the risks until she knew for sure. However, whoever has your chip still poses a risk to the general population. So, there's a hunt to find it."

"They didn't tell me right away. Neither did she."

"Naomi doesn't want you to view yourself as a weapon of mass destruction."

"Even if I am?"

"Even if you were, she'd help you find a way around it."

"Does that matter to you at all? If I end up being dangerous?"

"Looking at your body and the training you've had here, you're already dangerous. That doesn't intimidate me."

I laughed.

"We'd find a way. You'd find a way. No matter what."

Chapter Thirty-Nine

Over the course of the next few weeks Indigo stayed with me.

In that time, we trained together. He only went easy on me at first, before I flipped him over my shoulder in Clete fashion. Then he took me seriously. I laughed more than bare hand fighting or weapon's training normally warrants.

We ate our meals together. He was in my shop while I worked on designs and tattoos. Indigo even started to draw again. Which he hadn't done since before I ran away. While much of his work was sloppy, I found it endearing. We both could fill that silence with our own work and interpretations. We slept in my hut, him taking the lone bed Naomi left behind. The other women stared and whispered at times, but I didn't mind.

We stargazed again like we did as children. But we spoke of the day's events as well as the tasks to come. He no longer tried to foresee my future.

Always at the tip of my tongue was the question I longed to ask. The answer to which I was aching harder each day to know. Even if it hurt. Even if it scared me. Even if I didn't know what to do with it. Indigo found plenty of things to say to me to keep the gaps of silence from becoming too wide. Yet his eyes attempted to coax more out of me. Quietly attempting to get me to ask what he already knew I wanted to.

Still, I couldn't

***

The day came that I couldn't take it anymore. Before we left my hut, I grabbed his arm.

"Wait." I said.

He stopped and turned. But didn't say anything.

"What do you really want with me?"

"Truthfully," he paused. I could see the Orca tattoo I designed for him on his arm. As he placed his hand over mine. He looked away for a moment to the ground. Then he looked straight into me.

"I love you."

I froze in place.

"Yeah." I replied.

He didn't say anything else for a while as he stood there in place.

Finally, he turned my face to his.

"I mean it. I love you. I always have."

I looked to the floor. Yet I still felt his gaze.

"Can you at least tell me you understand what I'm saying?"

I didn't answer.

"Look at me."

My eyes met his. The intensity burned through me.

"Everything in my life has been driven by my undying love for you. Even if it's not mutual, you're the most important person to my whole world. I can live with that. I've already lived with it being one sided for most of my life. But what I can't live with is not knowing how you feel about me. I promise whatever is true, I'll respect it. I need to know though."

"Indigo."

"Sky."

"I don't have an answer for you."

"Sky, after all these years you know if you love me or if you don't. There's no not knowing here."

I couldn't speak. He sighed.

"Sky, I need to know if it's time for me to go back to Wild Dog or stay here with you."

"Indigo, you've always deserved so much more than what I gave you. You tried so hard and meanwhile I was just a mess. I could still be a weapon and...."

I stopped myself.

"We'll talk about this again at nightfall."

I walked off to the woods.

Chapter Forty

Sooner than I thought I would, I made it to the tree of life. I hadn't brought Indigo here yet, but I wanted to. I wanted to share my whole world with him still. My whole life.

I rested my head against the bark, hugged myself into the tree, and closed my eyes. I called to whoever Andromeda had been calling to the first night I came here.

I deflected the whole situation with Indigo before. I realized I'm comfortable with infatuation. Especially when it's one sided on my end. But this? I'm wasn't sure how to handle it at all. Every romantic stirring in my life lead to something terrible.

Except with Indigo.

***

Those feelings ran deeper than anything else. Deeper than my teenage hormonal crush on Conroy. Deeper that the artificial and technological connection Aziel created between us. Deeper than anything else in my life.

I could probably even leave everything now if I really wanted to. Abandon Infinity. Run away from Indigo once more. Deal with whatever happened with the chip. Hide myself from the rest of the world. But I didn't want to. I enjoyed who I was here. What I was becoming. What I was finding in myself. My art had taken on a whole new life. I was creating more than ever. I had meaning and purpose amongst the women here. Not just as a warrior, but as a comrade and individual.

And I had a man who loved me.

Who I loved back.

But what if I did become a danger to everything I now held so dear?

"Sky." I heard a whisper which echoed with a musical chime.

I turned around.

A woman in a short white gossamer dress stood before me. Her whole body glowed, despite the cloudy air. Her eyes were silver and reminded me of the moon. She held a bow and arrow in her right hand, and a deer stood next to her to her right. Her auburn hair flowed towards the deer.

I gasped. I'd never seen a more beautiful woman in my entire life.

I recognized her as Artemis. I'd painted her before, but the paintings paled compared to seeing the real thing.

We stood there staring at each other for a while. That beautiful comforting silence communicated everything that needed to be.

Then her and the doe walked off and vanished into the trees.

***

I felt the rain coming, so I ran towards home. A few drops landed on me as I followed my heart to my workshop. Once I made it inside, the clouds unleashed their bounty, rain drummed loudly on my roof.

Indigo sat next to the center table, sketching. He met my gaze for only a moment, before returning his eyes to the image before him. I stood there watching him for a few moments.

This wasn't how I was letting this go. Not any longer.

"Indigo."

His eyes were on mine again.

I approached Indigo and pulled him to his feet. His face revealed his shock.

Before he had the chance to say my name, I kissed him. For a moment all I heard was the rain. He didn't hesitate for long though, as I felt his hands begin to gently explore my back. His gaze reached into mine just to make sure this was what I wanted. I nodded. Then his physical motions proved as swift and strong as mine. We made our way back down to the earth itself. He made his way on top of me, taking off the layers between us.

***

Soon I don't know where he began, and I ended. Our worlds were finally one. No longer were there walls between us. We were feeling the connection we always had. So ingrained was it into who we were nothing could break it. No matter the distance, the years that went by, or the choices we made. I was just finally realizing it.

I felt Indigo reach my deepest parts. It all felt familiar somehow. He's blue inside just like me. Not from drugs or implants. But in the way beyond what could be seen. Beyond what could be expressed, yet we understood.

We reached to each other to stay close into each other's worlds. Not just physically. But a kinship I'd never shared with another human being. I never would share this with anyone else. Half of me had always belonged to Indigo and half of him had always been mine. We'd felt each other's paths even when we were torn apart. Even if we didn't realize at the time. We were destined to find our way back to each other. We'd always been reaching to each other. Not in trying to find ourselves or completing ourselves. But in working to reach something higher by finding our way.

I hadn't been intimate with another in so long. For the first time, this intimacy was something of my choosing. Not something forced upon me or that I fell into. Not some strange power play or urge with little backing. I was choosing Indigo. This is what my heart wanted, and he was choosing me back. Not to satisfy some selfish need. But to fulfill me and be with me in the most intimate way possible.

This was the first time I was truly making love. Truly feeling whole with another human being. Not just sexual pleasure but feeling my full being connect with the vulnerabilities and love of another.

Indigo took all of me in. I felt him warmly move on every part. Without hesitation. Without holding back. I was experiencing for the first time what it's like for a man to give himself fully.

***

We rested for a while and listened to the rain. My fingers drew shapes across Indigo's chest. He held me close.

"Was that your answer?" Indigo asked.

"It was easier to show you then say it the first time."

"I can understand that."

"You'll stay with me here? Wild Dog won't have a problem with that?"

"He's reasonable. We'll work something out."

"You sure?"

"Yeah."

My head sunk into his chest.

I wanted an eternity to take this all in. As I stared at the ceiling of my workshop, my world felt finally whole.

"Sky."

But before Indigo can finished, we heard a commotion outside. Shouts and heavy footsteps trembled the earth itself.

"Andromeda is dying!"

Chapter Forty-One

Indigo and I dressed in haste and exited the tent.

Andromeda was on a stretcher being brought back to her medical hut. Her hair was lying about and covering her face.

Clete followed close behind. Her face was blank, but in her eyes, I saw the deep love she held for her. She followed Andromeda into the hut.

I heard women crying. Two of had passed in battle. I felt that before my currents told me so.

But I hadn't even known we were in battle before.

"Sky." I heard Wolf call.

"What happened?" I asked once we were face to face.

"We were closing in on the location of the chip. We'd made it to the island and didn't see any guards or warriors around. We weren't sure if there was an ambush on the way or something else entirely. There wasn't a cloud in the sky. Yet lightning shot out from the land itself. Those of us covered in the most seawater got the worst of it."

More wounded passed us on stretchers heading to the medical huts.

"Why did they just approach it like that? Naomi I'm sure told them the chip itself possessed danger. It releases currents itself."

"Andromeda through a tiny infiltration without alerting the occupants would keep it from sending an attack."

"The chip can sense anything living nearby!"

"We didn't know that."

"Well it couldn't before. It can now."

I realized the changes of the currents within me also mirrored the chip which no longer belonged to me. True, before I could only feel Aziel with it. Now, I could feel other beings as well. With the chip doing the same, it made it even more dangerous.

I ran to Andromeda's hut. Indigo followed.

***

Andromeda lay on the bed, unconscious while her mind seemed light years away. I couldn't approach her about this, not now.

Clete rose and met me and Indigo.

"What is it?"

"Why didn't Andromeda and the others consult me on the chip? We could have prevented all of this."

"Your chip might still have a track on you. Anything you knew about our plans; the chip could be able to get a hold of as well and provide that information to whoever is carrying it. Knowing the chip knew we knew of its location and were soon on the way was bad enough. But hiding the rest of the information gave us a better chance of finding it and destroying it."

Clete turned her attention to Indigo.

"Wild Dog and some of the others are on the way."

"Our joint efforts will be more than enough to defeat whatever we're facing." Indigo replied.

"Let's not underestimate it though. We've already seen what that's cost us." Clete turned to Andromeda.

"I think it's best you two leave. The medical team will be back, and this hut will become too crowded. I'll address you when it's time."

Indigo led me back to my hut.

***

Indigo fell asleep on my chest as I stared at the ceiling. Our first night sharing a bed should have been a lot sweeter. But a weight held down my whole being. I stroked his hair.

They all needed me now for this mission. Get to the chip and destroy it. I was the only one who was resistant to its charge. My body built up to handle it. Infinity still felt I'm too young for combat, but I didn't think they couldn't defeat it on their own.

Before bed, Indigo spoke of using a possible worm to hack it and shut it down. He said there were many ways to deal with the chip. I told him to stop talking about it. I still wasn't sure if any plots were being tracked through me by the chip.

But what if they didn't ask me? What if they didn't see me as trustworthy? Feared the chip would play mind control on me as well? They said it themselves, there was still a chance the chip could cause my body to go haywire. I could kill everyone just by staying put. Yet they refused to exile me.

What if they sent someone else to die?

Like Indigo.

I held him tight.

I couldn't let that happen. I had to go alone and deal with this. It couldn't until Wild Dog got here. I couldn't risk them not sending me and sending others to die instead. Especially Indigo.

Indigo was going to think I was running away again. Betraying him after finally feeling we could have a future together. But I didn't have any other choice.

I called out to the chip.

Chapter Forty-Two

I didn't pack anything this time. I didn't need to. I wasn't running away this time. I was going to make it back.

The rain stopped before I made my ways into the forest. I knew my way around these parts now. Knew the individual trees and paths. Though I still wasn't able to map my location based on the sky. I would pass the Tree of Life to gather strength before heading to the ocean.

I could feel the chip calling back to me. Pulling me towards it. It wanted to be found but by me and me alone. It wanted to reunite with me. Be part of me again. I was feeling nauseous, but I kept moving towards it. I vowed to destroy that thing, so it could never speak to me again. It didn't seem to have a response to my darker feelings about it. I did my best to hide it from the chip. It just kept calling.

My hand brushed against the tree of life as I walked past it. That was more than enough to give me the nerve to keep going.

Problem was, I realized there was an ocean between us which I couldn't simply swim across. I hadn't thought about dealing with the body of water since I left in such haste. I cursed at my own stupidity. I closed my eyes and called to the Goddess I'd seen near at the Tree of Life as loud as my voice would go.

"Artemis!"

But she didn't appear. I heard nothing in response.

Perhaps she had been a hallucination all along.

But then I saw lights emerging from the waters. Dark fins poked out from the waves and heading towards me. Two orcas beached themselves before me. I ran towards them, only slowing my feet when I saw elongated fins lifting their bodies slighting into the air.

These were the cyborg orcas from my dreams. Exactly the same ones. They weren't just a dream after all.

Did Artemis send these Cyborcas? That would have been an interesting way to answer my prayers. But I guess Goddesses kept up with the times as well. Or perhaps they felt my currents instead. Maybe it was a mixture of both.

I ran into the ocean to meet them. Making eye contact, I could feel them communicating with me as well. The one to my right told me to hop on top of her.

I tried to explain I couldn't breathe underwater. Slowly they made their way into deeper water, first crawling over the sand with their bottom fins then back to swimming with their fins once the water was deep enough. It didn't seem the Cyborca was responding to my fears and took a dive under. I didn't even get a chance to take a breath. I was about to let go to swim to the surface when I saw she developed an air pocket for me. It was emerging from her blowhole and I brought my face into it. I was able to breathe and see clearly underwater.

The world around me was so alien. More alien than the pictures I've seen coming back from Mars, Enceladus, and all of the Exo-planets combined. We didn't need to go into space to find aliens. They were already down here.

The fish themselves were in an array of colors and shapes. Some even seemed to have creatures of their own growing as part of them. These weren't species originally found in this area but must had evolved to make it everywhere else. Developed new parts in order to survive these new worlds. Nature's own cyborgs. I laughed at the idea and almost choked before I re-aligned myself with the air bubble.

I saw the same features on the Cyborcas I'd seen in my dreams. Goggled eyes. Replaced fins and tails. Extra limbs.

Natural orcas swam alongside us as well. I touched one as a comparison to the cyborg. Both were rubbery, except for the synthetic parts. Yet their spirits felt the same. They belonged to the same pack and nothing would change that. I could feel their loyalties to one another. Their love.

Questions from my old dream returned. How did they become like this? Was this done to them and they survived despite it? Or had they found a way to do this to themselves to survive? But it didn't seem to matter what had been modified, they were still going about life as Orcas. I kept feeling the others who passed me, letting my fingers brush against them as they swam by.

I felt my own skin after that. First my hand and then my navel, where the scar remained.

I realized now I was a cyborg. Forever touched and altered by technology. But that didn't mean I didn't belong to the natural world. Earth was still mine. Between the natural world and the technological age, my destiny was still my own.

Part of me wanted to stay in this world forever, among these aliens and cyborgs.

But we reached the point where the Orcas could go no further. The one I was riding pulled me to the beach. I dismounted and felt my feet once again on earthly floor. Being suspended in water for so long had left me slightly dizzy. I turned around and kissed the top of its head. I heard it crackle and chirp in response before it used it's extended synthetic legs to get itself back in the ocean. I watch the fins until they'd all vanished into the water.

I wasn't sure if I properly communicated my gratitude, but it was too late now. Unless they still picked up my transmission from far away.

The sand quickly turned to rock as I walked towards the concrete building before me. It was dark grey and blended with the surrounding rock. It reminded me of a castle. Not one of the past, but a fortress looking to stand its ground in a dark future.

One which I wouldn't let happen.

I used my chip to heat my body, so my clothes dried. Then I felt for the chip. It seemed more eager in its calling now that I was close. I could feel its location clearly now. I approached.

Chapter Forty-Three

Being back in the world of concrete freaked me out at first. I didn't feel like the same person anymore who came from this world. But somewhere inside that girl remained. I needed her now if I had any hope of getting through this alive. She was always so much more than I gave her credit for. For she was the basis of the start of the warrior I was becoming. I wasn't quite her yet either. I was somewhere between the two women; finding myself. This cyborg could make it through these worlds.

I crouched in the darkness, doing my best to ensure nothing crunched underneath my feet. I don't see anyone else around. I sensed whoever else was here, was here alone. Why weren't there any guards? Was the chip that strong of a weapon to not need anyone else? It hadn't done anything to me yet, but I feared it could retaliate at any point. Take revenge for attempting to destroy it. But that was a risk I needed to take, or more would die.

It's a cylinder tower which my chip was calling me from. It was shorter than the others. I climbed a tree full of vines and snuck in through the window. There was no glass or bars covering it, which surprised me. There's no security around this chip. But when I looked down through the window, I saw the ground inside was far below where I was. It was going to be hard to get down without breaking all my bones or dying. However, I was able to pull one of the vines from the tower off and feed it into the window and work my way down.

Still, this was too easy. Something else had to be coming.

Inside the walls were also that same stone grey. Some of the stones had been artificial modified as a light source so I was able to see clearly. It appeared barren beyond that.

I thought it would be possible to return with the destroyed chip before anyone knew I was gone. Sure, I'd need to find a way to cross the ocean if the Cyborcas didn't return. But I was perfectly capable of figuring it out.

After I destroyed the chip. Which part of me no longer wanted to do?

Was I really starting to feel guilty about this?

The chip continued egging me towards a staircase which spiraled downward. I could feel it was close. My whole body tingled with charge.

The tingling sensation in my body overwhelmed me as I worked my way deeper into the earth and further into the building.

When I reach the chip, it was perched on a stand on a table. No glass or lock around it. No type of security around it at all. It was just perched there, vulnerable and helpless to my whim.

That piece of blue was no longer part of me. But I still felt its imprint deep within me. My imprint remained on it as well. My blood may have dried, but it's permanently stained that blue in places it would never come clean. The currents I felt off it were excitable, like a dog that had waited a long time to see its beloved master.

Its influence on my body and my life was undeniable. So much of what I was now was due to the chip. I second guessed if it was really right to terminate it. But I reminded myself it's just a piece of technology with no real thought of its own. It must have been reprogrammed to mess with me, so I wouldn't destroy it. It didn't really have feelings, but it knew how to manipulate mine. Those circuits no longer had any use to me, and no good use for anyone else with a conscious.

It almost killed me. It killed a Jackal. It killed women from my army. And it wouldn't think twice of killing anyone else.

That made up my mind.

I took the chip into my hand. I stroked it with my thumb. Then I started to send current from my body to fry the hardwire.

I felt a hand take hold of my shoulder.

"Aziel." I heard myself say as I turned around.

"I'm surprised in you," he said, "And disappointed." A shock ran through his hand into my shoulder and coursed through the rest of my body. I screamed in pain and I fell to floor.

Chapter Forty-Four

I felt as if I was choking on ice. I convulsed. Aziel sent calming currents into me and I gasped for air. My scrambled brain recentered itself. I looked up at him.

His hair had gotten longer, and his face seemed more etched in his features. There was also a scar across his cheek. He looked almost the same beyond that. His metallic eyes were as bright as ever.

How had I not felt him around? I always could catch him creeping up on me before. What was this? But then again, I hadn't felt him in years. How could I be so sure his cloaking abilities hadn't improved? After all, I'd been able to hide my currents from him long before I knew what I was doing with the chip. My abilities had changed, logically it would have been the same for him as well.

"You and I, we share something in common." Aziel said, "We are the only two people in the entire world who successfully survived our chips.

Naomi was right. Part of me already knew this to be true as well. I just didn't want to believe it at the time.

"I couldn't feel you on the way in." I managed to say.

"I had been calling to you for a while and you wouldn't come. So, I finally resorted to waking the chip so that it would call to you itself. I knew you wouldn't be able to resist. It's part of you. As mine is part of me."

"What do you mean? I haven't felt you in years."

"Your dreams? I know I got to you there. Perhaps you just didn't want to be found."

I had dreamed of Aziel quite often in the past few years. Yet I hadn't seen it as him trying to communicate with me. Rather, me facing my biggest fears and more complex emotions. Those dreams were him trying to contact me when my guard was down.

"I felt you fighting me while you were awake, so I knew I was going to need to coax me back. You didn't understand our connection, even though I could feel it. By getting close to me again and explaining everything, I knew I could alleviate the confusion and fear the situation created. End your distrust and bring you back to me."

"Why didn't you tell me you had one too?" I asked between gulps of air and pain surges. Currents from his first pass were keeping me too hurt to rise from the floor, despite the calming ones also coursing through.

"I didn't at that point. Mine was removed and the results remained. I was planning on telling you when Conroy and the others were dead, and you were safely under my wing. Then I was going to remove yours. See the remaining results. I do have to say, your acclimated abilities from the chip haven't been a disappointment. You responded better than I could have ever hoped."

"What do you mean?"

"You've been part of a much larger experiment. Conroy only knew the tip of the iceberg. He was too stupid to look beyond that."

Aziel lifted me to my feet, and then sat me into a chair next to where the chip had been perched.

"Stay there." He ordered.

My body was still too exhausted to disobey. But my mind was still ready to fight. It wanted nothing more than to take him down.

"Yeah. An experiment you refused to tell me anything about."

"Now you'll know everything. The further delay in giving you that information was beyond my control. You were the one who wandered off and got yourself captured, if you don't remember. I told you to stay put."

"Too little too late to make it up to me. Plus, you didn't prove yourself to be too trustworthy."

Aziel laughed. Was this a joke to him?

"For most people I'm not. But for you? There's never been a reason for you to fear me. Oh, I've missed you, Sky. Have you missed me too? I know what you experienced with me won't happen with anyone else. The feeling is mutual. We won't get those electric highs off anyone else."

"I wouldn't get too cocky." I said back.

He shocked me again. My vision turned white as I felt lit on fire. But just as quickly it was all over.

"I also can hurt you like no one else can."

I wanted to kill him.

"But time in those armies probably amplified the fight in you. That's going to be useful towards others, but not me."

I really wanted to kill him.

Aziel circled around me and inspected my body.

"You're stronger now. That's good. And what happened to the blue in your hair?"

He lifted parts of my hair for a closer look. Every fiber of my being wanted to punch him.

"I can see that's diminished. You're not the little girl I left you as. You're a full-grown woman."

"You never knew me as a little girl, Aziel."

"I'm not liking this attitude you're having towards me. You like me, remember? Perhaps too many years apart made you fear I'd abandoned you. It would explain why you shut yourself off to me and were so hard to find. But I've never forgotten you, Sky. For all these years, my sole goal was finding you."

"Why? So you could control me again?"

"So we can rebuild the world to our will, and no one else's."

"I've heard that mantra before. You're no better than Conroy."

"Don't you dare compare me to him," His voice hurt my whole body, "His gang was a joke and meanwhile you managed to get yourself wrapped up in that. You were always so far beyond any of them. It disgusted me to see you put yourself in the same category. Though I'm not sure how I would have found you in the first place without them. So perhaps it was just a necessary twist of fate to get us on the right track."

Aziel took a breath. His silver eyes burrowed into mine.

"Let me enlighten you, and I'm sure you'll be on my side. As you always should have been. You always were supposed to be mine. And now you will be."

He ran a calming current into me as his hands gently tangled themselves into my hair.

"I just need to get you to see that. We have a purpose and a mission together, you and I."

"You want to make a new world with me, Aziel?"

"Yes. We'll have more than you could have ever imagined."

***

"You and I have a rare genetic mutation which allows our cells to live alongside technology in perfect harmony. Most people develop cancers or die of heart failure soon after the inserting of the chip. Everyone else but us. Our bodies can handle it just fine. In fact, we thrive on it. We are the people of the future. Of the new generation. Our spawn will repopulate and control the whole world one day. This is the future, bridging the miracle of the human species and technology into one."

"And if I refuse?"

"There is no refusal unless you decide on a life of slavery. Other fighting forces will find ways to take advantage of you instead. Not understanding how special and precious you truly are, only seeing you as a tool in their game. Your abilities are to be used regardless. It's best to stick with me and get the chance to use them yourself."

"The last two armies I was involved with didn't use me at all."

"You sure about that? Your first captors took your chip after all. They didn't destroy it. Why not if they had no use for it?"

"Perhaps to develop better means of self-defense in case there were any more out there?"

"That would be perfectly redeemable if it was true. But it wasn't. You see I was able to break into the lab of the Jackals by hacking into your chip. I was simply trying to find you at the time, but instead I learned you'd been long moved and took the opportunity to gather some intel. Doctor Naomi was developing a super weapon under the orders of Wild Dog. You didn't have any idea, did you? But the chip couldn't be used for such a purpose any longer. Besides some minor defense mechanisms, it had released the best of itself into you. Your body adapted around the rest and developed itself beyond what the chip was ever capable of. They didn't realize the extent the technology changed you on the inside. Not at first. You're the real weapon."

"Then why would they feel the need to go after it? It killed one of the Jackals! It killed women from my army."

"The chip didn't kill them, I did. Our currents are deadly to everyone else, my dear. It was necessary to kill them. And I'm going to need to kill the rest of them to ensure you're finally safe. Take vengeance for everything they did to you. The years they took away from us. All so they could use you as a pawn for their own warfare."

"That's a lie!"

"Just because you don't want it to be the truth, doesn't make it any less real. Anyone else out there will use you. The only one you can trust is me."

"You want me to trust you so that you may use me as a weapon instead."

"I wish to rule you, so we can co-rule the rest of the world. So that we both can experience our powers to the greatest of our abilities. The world we've been brought into is harsh without mercy. But we have an advantage over the rest. We're the weapons of the future."

"I've been a lot of things, Aziel. Street rat, gang member, and criminal among them. But I was never a killer. And I don't plan on becoming one now."

"That may be true that you were never a killer before. But the chip turned you into a lethal weapon. This chip permanently altered your body. You could also describe a psychic power which came with it as well. One that runs on electric currents. You can pick up, influence, and create your own currents. Whether it's from the sky, a computer, or even the currents within the human body and mind. In time you could influence many at once. Inside of you is the power potential beyond that of an atomic bomb. Once you've mastered your currents, the rest of the world will be beneath you. You can leave generations with cancer. Destroy whole planets. Redirect cyber controlled weapons. The world will be at your mercy and will."

"I don't have to be defined by any of that."

"As much as you may be my little angel, you're a demon inside too."

"I refuse to be a weapon."

"Denial doesn't change who you are. Both armies you were involved with had great plans for you. Yet you are avoiding your own power. I've used my powers. Why not take advantage of them yourself?"

"Can I use them so that you'll let me go and leave me alone for the rest of my life?"

"Don't make jokes. Not now. Not when I'm finally able to tell you everything. This should have happened years ago."

This was sounding life crazy science fiction to me. Perhaps his own chip caused some haywire in his own brain. Frying his mind like a toaster in a bathtub.

If that was my captor, I needed to get out of this fast.

***

The situation was so surreal for me, that I was experiencing an almost out of body like sensation. It could have been one too many shocks from Aziel, because I was sure I was missing critical information he was finally sharing with me. Ironic wasn't it? I spent years longing for answers, and when I no longer cared; I was finally receiving them. I wasn't even hearing half of them. I let him drabble on while I attempting to form together an escape plan.

"I was never aligned with that gang you were stuck in. No, they were pawns in a much bigger game of mine. They were going extinct. They weren't evolving fast enough to reach the future. Most of the world isn't. Unlike us. I simply sped up their demise. I provided one of the Jackals with fake intel on your whereabouts which he believed so quickly, and he never even took a look into it at all. He was too trusting of me. I wasn't sure why he was so eager to find you beyond your potential use in warfare, but perhaps I was reading too far into it. He ended up in the hands of Conroy's gang and burned alive in one of their experimental chemical fires."

I didn't tell Aziel that not only had Indigo survived the fire, I had been the one to save him. I let him continue.

"Though I became impatient on how long it would take for the Jackals to retaliate and did in Conroy's gang myself. So, I told Conroy I had intel on your location and needed every last one of his remaining members to meet in order to develop the plan to capture you. On the outside looking in, I'd never done wrong by him. But underneath the surface, Conroy was only becoming my tool. When he was no longer useful I caused the whole operation to self-destruct. I electrocuted them myself when I went back to their base. Their guns went off like fireworks. But I'd miscalculated the amount of current it would take to kill them all. It left me utterly exhausted and powerless for quite a while. I didn't have the strength to make my way back to you. I slept in one of their secret compartments for quite a few days, only being awoken by the smell of dead body's when the fumes reached their climax."

"Staying put would have screwed me over anyway?"

"I would have called to you with the chip and directed you until I could make it back. But I felt you moved and was unable to locate you until I'd managed to recharge."

"You didn't need to kill them all, Aziel."

"They were planning to kill you, you're aware of that?"

"Yes."

"Do you know why?"

"No."

"Your artwork."

"What?"

"Yes, I know. I was shocked too."

"But why?"

"Whenever you stay in certain places for long period of time, you leave traces of yourself behind. The chip with it. Your graffiti art drew attention to those spots. Once you left a spot, often the charge would diminish within a few hours. Unless the area was high in quartz or your paints. The ingredients in paint has changed dramatically over the years, even though most people didn't even know it was altered at all. Certain materials are simply cheaper and easier to attain for the same effect. Since most street artists are poor, it made sense to switch to these materials. But they happen to last better than old fashioned paints. They're also full of materials which record technological and electronic spikes. Like yours."

I stammered. Really, my painting had been what put my life on the line in the end? I know I would have risked my life to paint, but I didn't realize how it had put me in danger.

Aziel continued. "The police started figuring it out. They were looking to catch you. Not for the art itself, but to get a hold of your illegal technology. They didn't know about your chip per say, but they knew a civilian and criminal had a hold of technology they could have never gotten clearance to attain. They wanted to detain and question you. See if you were part of some smuggling ring. Or an illegal experiment."

"Why didn't the gang tell me?"

"They're scum. They didn't see a need when they decided it was best to eliminate you instead."

I gasped and stare at the floor. The news still shocked me somehow.

"Conroy…"

"Wasn't interested in saving you any longer. Despite me reminding him of the importance of the technology inside of you. Hence why it became absolutely necessary for me to terminate them all myself. You weren't strong enough to do the job on your own yet."

"I wouldn't have killed them."

"With your life on the line, I highly doubt that. Anyway, it's been years since you painted in the city. Traces of your electric imprints are long gone. The trail they had on you has gone cold. It's a good thing you gave up your painting. It would have killed you in the end."

"And you're not?"

"No."

"That chip could have killed me too you know. What makes you any better?"

"I knew it wouldn't because we have the same mutation, and I've already saw it worked within myself. There was no risk to you as long at the chip was removed in time."

"There was no guarantee of that. You said it yourself that the others who went through the process died from it early on. What's to say we just don't have a delayed effect? It could still end up killing us both later."

"You're arguing against science?"

"Scientific studies have proven to be wrong over and over again."

"Last I checked, gravity was still a thing."

"My skin was turning blue. I was dying!"

"If you had stayed put the day I told you to, that wouldn't have been an issue."

"You said yourself you didn't have the strength to get back to me! The Jackals saved me when you couldn't."

Aziel slapped me. I cracked my jaw in response. He sighed again.

"You're right. I failed you. But something like that won't happen again. I have a better understanding of my powers now. And I'll help you better understand yours. We won't have to worry about getting separated again. Rest now."

He walked off.

Chapter Forty-Five

I slept for a short while. The sound of Aziel's feet woke me and I remembered the nightmare I was stuck in. I calmed myself. My head was clear now. No longer lethargic from the currents he'd sent through me. The more information I gathered, the better chance I had getting out of this.

"How did you end up with the chip?" I asked.

"I thought I'd shown you some of that after the surgery."

"So those images were real memories."

"Yes. I was part of an organization which has since crumbled due to their government being wiped out. XF. I was drawn into them as a child since they discovered the mutation within me. A doctor had found it during a routine exam when a computer server picked it up. He was eliminated soon after by XF. My family willingly gave me up for a large sum, only to be assassinated a few nights later to ensure they didn't talk. I was experimented on day after day. I didn't know any sense of privacy, joy, or innocence as a child. They tried and failed at developing technology off my body. That is, until the development of the chip. It turned the body into its own conduit, making it able to produce and control electronic currents as well as cyber ones. The version I had was much more archaic compared to yours. Your abilities already surpassed where I was at your age."

I doubted Aziel was much older than me. Yet he carried so much from his past which had aged him so much. My currents told me he felt hundreds of years old.

"Later they trained me as a spy. I rose through the ranks and became an asset, not just for my mutation but my ability at gathering intel and manipulating the enemy. My mission became to find more of my kind. More of us with the genetic mutation. That remained my purpose in life even after XF was disbanded. Year after year I searched and found nothing. For a long time, I thought I was the only one of my kind. Until I found you."

He placed his hand over my forehead. I suddenly flashed to an old memory. Not mine. But his.

I'd been painting a Pegasus flying through the clouds. He'd been walking by, after an assassination, and happened to see me as he was sneaking through the labyrinth of tunnels the cops had yet to figure out. He wasn't sure why. But I intrigued him somehow. He was enchanted as I drew up those rainbow tinted wings in that blue sky. Hypnotized as I made life seemingly spring from nowhere. But he figured out why he was drawn to me. A hum. He had finally found someone with the same electronic connection. He watched me for a long time. Waiting for my eyes to become visible to him. I was so drawn into my artistic world, I didn't see him and didn't lift my gaze away from my work. Only after I finished did I turn around. That's when he saw my eyes and knew for sure I had the genetic mutation. The giveaway was multicolored eyes within the cool colored spectrum. His eyes were similar before he disguised them as silver.

I only remembered creating the Pegasus. Nothing else. I hadn't realized how vulnerable I'd been while painting. How someone, anyone, could be watching me. How easy it would have been to pick me off.

"They were planning to do it while you were painting. They thought that would be the easiest time to take you out." Aziel's hand was still on my forehead. He'd read my thoughts. He lifted his hand away.

"Is that how you were able to take mind control of the Jackal?" I asked.

"I couldn't sneak into the lab, but I was able to coax the weaker minded of the group to touch the chip. I was able to control him from there. Mind control is harder than sci-fi stories make it out to be. Few people in his position are vulnerable enough to be taken over like that."

Then he leaned in and whispered into my ear, "But it did work on Conroy. I managed to get him to help me kill off the rest of his own gang."

"I thought you said you electrocuted them yourself."

"Conroy had locked everyone inside after I left the building. He shot rounds while I sent the currents to kill the others. Even as he was dying, he murdered many. Then I had him shoot himself. I thought it was a kind mercy after burning through his body with electricity. It was more than he deserved in the end."

I started to cry. Aziel tried to wipe my tears, but I turned my head away.

"You'll long for my touch again, just like you use to. In time you'll open to me again. You'll understand everything I've done for you. There are times lives need to end so the worthy ones can be spared."

***

"You could have told me from the start about the chip. There was no reason not to," I said through tears, "There was no reason to drag them into all this. I would have left them sooner had I known their fate.

"Your gang was particularly stupid. If you said anything to them it would have screwed us over. If you told the wrong person, you could have been found out sooner."

"I didn't have any friends at the time."

"You do now?"

I didn't answer. His silver eyes burrowed into mine.

He continued. "It's easy for something like that to slip out to the wrong person. And if you've been getting comfortable with anyone else recently, it's best you didn't gather this information until now."

"Is that not the only reason? You weren't afraid I'd ruin your ambition myself?"

"It's not like you would have been able to stop the changes from taking place. Once it was clear the armies were planning on using you and not killing you, I bided my time in getting you back. Their impossible to infiltrate by normal means. I'll give them that."

"Why were you willing to do this to me, Aziel? You had suffered through the procedure. It had also caused you great pain. Why put me through that too? You changed me against my will! Without my consent and for your own benefit."

"I was enhancing a quality already within you. There's great sacrifice that comes with great reward. It pained me to see what you were going through. It brought back old memories from my childhood, which I attempted to share to comfort you. I couldn't tell you what greatness was waiting on the other side of it all. Especially after you tried to remove it yourself, I almost laid my heart and soul to you. Unlike those who did it to me in FX, I cared about you. You're the most important thing in my whole life. I wanted to tell you all that. But I couldn't. Otherwise the others would get suspicious that the chip was more than what I told them it was."

"What did the gang think it was? A tracker device? Those have been implanted in people for years."

"I had to tell them it was a weapon. But I downplayed it. I knew I was going to kill them all anyway, and I could at least trust Conroy not to talk about it until then. I had an iron grip on his brain."

"It still could have killed me, Aziel."

"The only risk came after that army abducted you. But that's past us now. It can't hurt you anymore."

"What's to say there isn't anything else you don't know about this chip? We're glorified lab rats. You can't know everything this chip is doing to us."

"We're together in those unknown variables then, now aren't we? All the more reason to stick together."

"Why didn't you give me the choice?" My tears were returning. I hated that.

"As I mentioned, your mutation is so rare that I haven't found another with it. I couldn't risk you saying no or worse yet, getting away from me. Either way, I was putting that chip in you. It would have been a disservice to not let you be everything you could be."

"You didn't want to be alone anymore either." The words slipped out of my mouth.

"Both are true. You needed to be who you are to handle the chip. To deserve the power which comes with it. No longer having to be in solitude has ended a pain in me which I've carried all my life. Through every experiment, every personal betrayal, every mission."

I thought about that for a moment. How hard it must have been to be experimented on from such a young age. For your own family to not only neglect you but sell you away to some unknown and likely horrible fate. To have a piece of technology within you that was literally changing you from the inside in ways the body couldn't comprehend. Not having anyone else who understood. Only those who wished to gather knowledge or advantage through you. Without compassion or pity.

Aziel eyes met mine with a sadness I'd never seen from him before. I could see a touch of blue in them. In that moment he communicated with me everything he'd been forced to endure alone for all those years. Painful memories he carried day after day.

But why bring someone else into that world with those variables? It was selfish. Nothing could excuse one person choosing to inflict their pain on another.

Yet it made sense why he wanted to change the world.

As much as I wanted to run away from it, as much as I disagreed with what he'd done, there was a strong connection between Aziel and I. Even if it was artificial. Even if he'd been the one to create it. A pull I'd feel towards him for the rest of my life.

Was I doomed to suffer in that prison? Even if I managed to escape him? Forever trapped in the cyber cage he created just so he wouldn't suffer alone? Perhaps death would free us both.

No. I wouldn't let my mind go there. For now, I had to keep him talking. Figure out as much about my situation as I could.

"Was it from the drugs my parents took before I was born? The MX?"

"No. MX simplifies the workings of the body, not enhances it. The heightened concentration comes from repressing other aspects of the body and mind. The mutation is all you. Perfect you. But truthfully no one knows what causes the mutation. It's still a mystery. However, based on my research, we can most likely pass it our mutation on to the next generation through natural means. They might not even need to have the chip at all. They could easily surpass us in that regard."

"Is that what you really want? Children to surpass you? Won't that be a treat?"

"I, we, will teach them loyalty."

"So they'll be another tool then. Sounds like a perfectly functional family unit."

"Families find uses for each other or they fall apart. You should already know that."

"I thought you were sterile."

"I am. But there are ways to get around that."

"And if they don't share our traits?"

"We'll try a few more times and kill anyone who doesn't share those traits. We can always clone ourselves instead. Raising miniature copies of ourselves. Wouldn't that be wonderful?"

My stomach churned with acid.

"Dooming a whole new generation to the same fate."

"It's a gift. Not a curse. You've received great benefits from the chip yourself. And so will they."

He put his hand next to my ear and started to stroke my face.

"Even if cloning is the route we need to take, it doesn't mean we'd have to stop enjoying each other."

He rans another calming current as he touched me. Part of me enjoyed the sensation. I thought back to when he had pinned me against the wall, as our currents ran over each other. Nothing else made me feel that way. I was even longing for his currents after he drew his hand away. I wanted him all over me again. He gave me a triumphant smile.

"For years, I watched you eye Conroy like some god, which sickened me. He and his gang were so low on the totem pole compared to everything else going on. But I knew that was the yearnings of a naive girl who yet to experience someone who truly loved her. A girl who held a power she didn't know she had, while searching for it in others. I knew the chip would turn those affections towards me. After it was implanted, I knew you could feel the surge between us. I was finally connecting to another human in a way no one else ever had before. Finally had someone who loved me, and that feeling couldn't be altered or changed. Conroy could feel you turning your affections towards me instead. A connection between us he couldn't begin to fathom or destroy. He couldn't stand that you were finally falling for a real man. He didn't say it, but I knew exactly what he was feeling, and I took great pleasure in it. Conroy found it easier to resent you in turn."

"Not because he knew he'd aided in turning me into a weapon of mass destruction? Perhaps he felt some guilt."

"Conroy feeling guilty? Considering how many people died getting the synthetic implants and grafts, I doubt he was capable of such thing."

"He allowed people to stop getting them once he saw what was happening."

"Why are you defending him now? He's been dead for years and he wouldn't have done the same for you. He was in fact part of a plot to destroy you. Or have you forgotten already?"

The vessels in Aziel's neck were popping out.

"Based on what I know about Conroy, he probably wanted to destroy the weapon I'd become. He may have realized later how dangerous this situation could get. I doubt it was personal."

Aziel's hands were on either side of my shoulders.

"But it was for me."

He kissed the top of my head. The currents he sent through my nerves sent to my brain both sensations of comfort and disgust.

Horrible thoughts then flooded into my mind.

When I wasn't being used for war, he would use me for his pleasure. Using currents to convince me I was enjoying myself. Then he'd use me to make more of us.

For a moment I was falling into despair. After everything I'd been through, despite all my training, I was kidnapped and taken by Aziel once again. He'd been able to take his hold over me just like he had years ago. I was still so weak against him. I was once again simply a tool. Bound by fate to the will of others. I would spend the rest of my days as a weapon of war and a sex slave. I was his whether I wanted to be or not.

No. Those were his currents talking. Not mine. I wasn't going to let this be my fate.

Chapter Forty-Six

Aziel's arms were around me and he was stroking my hair again. My body ached for him, even though parts of my mind begged for it all to stop. I told myself to keep fighting it. Remember those he killed. How he'd put me through the surgery and inserted the chip against my will. His plans to use me. How he'd been the one to almost kill Indigo. I didn't see a way out yet, but this didn't mean I wasn't going to find one.

I sensed someone trying to penetrate the building from outside. Most likely an ally of mine. I sensed who it was once I followed the currents, but I did my best to hide this knowledge from Aziel. It didn't seem like he'd picked up on it yet. I had to distract him in the meantime during the infiltration.

"Aziel, take me back to when I was twenty and you had my back against the wall. Feeling every part of me inside and out. No layers between. Our currents rippling into ecstasy upon ecstasy."

His silver eyes lit up. "I knew you'd see things my way. You just needed some comfort and explanation after everything you've been through. After what Conroy did to you, it must have been hard to face your feelings for me when you didn't know it was mutual. But I can show you again now."

Aziel untied me and pulled me out of the chair. Within moments, my back was against the wall. His whole body pressed into mine.

"You're my whole world, Sky. Things are going to be better now for both of us. We'll be finally whole. No one can take that from us now." Aziel whispered in my ear before kissing my neck.

A tear ran raced down my check and down the other side of my neck where he couldn't feel it. I use my currents to dry it away and to prevent any more from forming. I took a deep breath.

With both hands I cradled Aziel's face. His silver met my blue. His relief in feeling he'd convinced me of this fate. Feeling he could finally have a home and family in me. I pulled his lips to mine and kissed him.

I was taken back to the day we united. I was starting to ride those highs again. Our currents reacquainted and reawakening what they could bring out in each other. Our pleasures and power. Only we would ever share such sensations, such experiences, with each other. That wasn't just his channels telling me this, it is also what I knew.

He hands reached underneath and worked slowly until he made it to my bare breasts. I moaned. I was ready to beg for him to make his way into me again. But he wouldn't yet. Now that he had me, he wanted to savor each sensation. Make me ache for him with each touch until he decided it was time to fulfill my desires.

Let him have you. He deserves you. The world will be yours if you just let him rule you. His currents became voices in my head. Lies to control me. Aziel wanted to make them the truth so badly. It didn't matter if it was a switch of currents creating fake feelings. Toying with my emotions to his whim. Forcing me to love him against my will.

When his mouth returned to my neck, my line of vision was cleared to see behind him. Indigo was working his way towards us. His gun in hand.

Chapter Forty-Seven

His eyes met mine. Fury illuminated the purple of his eyes. The feelings of hurt and betrayal were clear across his face. He raised the gun towards Aziel and I. It pained me greatly. In turn I felt Aziel sending more calming currents through me. Though another tear still managed to escape. I couldn't even have the thoughts I wanted to have at the end or Indigo wouldn't be able to do what he needed to now. Otherwise Aziel would read my thoughts and stop him.

Indigo understood then and his expression changed.

"Shoot us." I mouthed to Indigo silently.

He shook his head is response. Aziel still didn't respond to Indigo, despite him being so close. All he could see, and feel was me. Aziel moved his head to the other side of my neck.

"Kill us." I mouthed to Indigo.

Indigo didn't move. Aziel's face moved in front of mine.

"Why are you crying?" Aziel asked.

But my eyes moved back to Aziel's a moment too late and he was alerted to someone behind him. He released me and turned to Indigo.

He zapped the gun out of Indigo's hand and it smashed against the wall, "I guess that gang was too incompetent to finish you off. I'll need to finish you instead."

Indigo kicked Aziel in the head. Aziel toppled over.

Aziel rose and recovered as if nothing had happened at all. He shot currents into Indigo which sent him right into the wall. Indigo got up quickly and dodged the trail of currents Aziel attempted to send his way. Aziel laughed.

"What made you think you had any chance against me?" Indigo moved to the left a moment too late and Aziel caught him with one of his currents. He landed on the floor.

Aziel shocked him between bits of laughter. I heard a cry out of Indigo which expressed a pain unbearable by human standards. His body fighting the forces doing everything to shut it down. His mind telling him to keep going when unconsciousness would bring sweet release. He tried to rise before Aziel shocked him into the floor again. Indigo was too weak to move now.

Aziel looked on with pleasure. His smile etched into my mind. It was the look of nightmares. Of pure evil. Any feelings I may have had for him, shut off in that moment. Even the connection through the chips was weakened to the point it was no longer clouding my mind. I got to my feet while Aziel wasn't looking. My eyes were only on Indigo.

I was about to watch Indigo die. He couldn't even look at me. He was struggling for breath. There was no relief for his pain, no mercy from Aziel as he released shock after shock into his body. Each more powerful than the last.

This is exactly why I'd come alone in the first place. To keep this from happening. To keep him from facing a force he didn't understand.

Now he was going to die. Unless I did something to stop this.

I didn't have a choice.

With all my strength, I sent a shock into Aziel. He turned around with a look of confusion in his eyes. Once he faced me I ran up to him and placed my hand over his chest, sending currents right into his heart. The pain registered in his brain immediately. I locked my blue on his silver. I watch his eyes change from disbelief, to anger, to sadness at the betrayal. His entire world shattered. His vision with me gone. His life ending just when he thought he'd finally attained the future he truly wanted. I felt every private feeling and pain, within his last moments. I saw all his personal relationship with his death with an intimacy no one else ever experienced, and I would never see again. He wanted me to see it all, know him full as no one else had before because they hadn't cared to. He saw my pain too which made him wonder why. Made him still feel for me despite all. His last thought was that why, before he collapsed on the floor.

Cyborgs were still mortal. Which came as a great relief for me.

Indigo wasn't moving. I felt his vitals before I even touch him. He was still alive. My heart burst with joy. I sent currents into him. After a minute of stillness, he stirred.

Indigo hugged me. I held him back tightly, as if I could better ensure the life stayed packed in his body. As if my love itself could ward away death. I heard the beautiful sound of his breathing. His heart beating fast against mine with the exhilaration of survival. I felt my tears against his shoulders. I didn't need to hide those from him.

"How did you get here?" He asked.

"I felt my way with the chip."

"You saved me again, Sky."

"How did you get here?"

"I followed my heart."

I laughed for a moment before bringing him closer to me. I didn't need an explanation beyond that.

Intuition was something so hard to measure. Some scientific studies managed to make some findings here and there to confirm it had basis in the real world and served a purpose in the survival game. But overall it remained a mystery on how it could possibly work. Perhaps it would never be understood. There never would be a chip or piece of technology which would be able to fully replicate that. No artificial way to recreate the power of love either.

Chapter Forty-Eight

Once Indigo gathered his strength, I returned to the chip which Aziel had returned to its perch. I could still feel it calling to me in that almost enthusiastic state. My heart was breaking. I didn't want to have to do this. But I knew that I had no choice.

I took the chip into my hand. It was still asking me to implant it back inside of me. Be part of me again. I stroked it once more. Trying to bring it comfort in its final moment. If such a thing was possible. As if it could really experience such things.

"I can do it instead if it's too much for you, Sky." Indigo said. He stood before me. The chip was now between us.

"No. I need to do this. For me." I looked down at that blue square for the last time.

I sent a charge of currents into the chip so powerful that it was fried instantly. It didn't have the chance to suffer if such a thing was possible from it. It was all over. The chip was silent, and I could feel it was dead. There was no coming back from that. I dropped it to the floor and crushed it under my foot, even though I knew it wasn't necessary.

The imprint would always remain deep in me. The scars it left in me inside and out, would forever remain. Even with its destruction, I would never be as I was before. I felt hollow then, but perhaps I could find a new wholeness in my new self.

"How do you feel?" Indigo asked.

"Sad but relieved, I don't know the rest yet."

"You don't have to. You don't ever have to."

I smiled. His indigo met my blue. There was the home and family I wanted to have.

***

I left with Indigo. He told me the Jackals would be arriving shortly to take care of the rest, but he had indeed arrived alone. We travelled by boat, the one he'd brought to get to me. I kept my eyes on the horizon between sea and sky. I felt Indigo's eyes turn to check on me between navigating us back to shore, occasionally waving at a passing Jackal boat to confirm his mission had been a success. Wild cries of triumph were their response as they made their way to the island.

Then I heard those lovely clicking sounds. The orcas were back and were riding alongside us. I reached my hand to stroke them. They cried happily in turn. Indigo stopped the boat and watched for a while. Cyborcas meshed perfectly with the others as they swam around us, me touching each one which came to pass. Indigo's smile communicated everything he could have said. I wondered to myself if there was such a thing as cyborg mermaids too.

Eventually he asked if we could continue home and I nodded. The orcas continued to follow us.

Indigo allowed me my silence. My eyes only met his occasionally. My hands keep running over those orca backs, feeling where flesh met machine. We didn't need any words. I was relieved not to deal with any words for the time being.

***

We reached land and Indigo led me back to my hut. He laid me on my bed and sat at the chair across from me.

"Naomi will be here shortly to check you out."

"Shouldn't she check you first? You were the one who almost died, not me."

"Honestly, whatever you did made me feel better than ever! I can wait until after for her to check me out."

Naomi entered the hut.

"Good to see you, Sky."

"Naomi." That was all I could say in return. She looked the same, apart from a subtle glow to her skin and sheen to her hair.

"Tell me where it hurts." She said.

I pointed to my naval where the chip use to be.

"I can still feel the imprint in me."

She sighed, "Unfortunately I won't be able to do much about that phantom pain the chip left behind. You'll likely feel that for the rest of your life."

"Do you have any updates on Andromeda?"

She nodded.

"I treated her when I got here. She's slowly recovering. Though it looked grim at first. She'd made arrangements with Clete just in case."

"Naomi saved her with her magic touch, as is her usual way." Indigo boasted.

Naomi blushed in turn. "There are others here who are trained well medically besides me. Andromeda's will kept her alive when all else looked bleak."

"I'm so happy she's going to be ok." I sighed in relief.

When Naomi finished our examinations, finding nothing which needed further testing, she left Indigo and I alone once more. Indigo crawled into my bed. I took shelter in his arms.

"You destroyed it. You're safe now." He whispered to me.

"Would it be better for me to destroy myself as well?"

"No," He turned his face towards mine, "Never. Sky, I never want you to say or believe anything like that ever again."

"I'm still a weapon of mass destruction."

"Not if you don't want to be."

"What if I'm forced to be?"

"No one can force you. What the chip did to you was against your will, but you can choose now what you do with the powers it gave you."

"What good can I be?"

"You can help others. Help all of us." Indigo told me softly. "You're also resistant to technologies now which can affect the rest of us. Naomi has already been using your blood to develop a vaccine which has been doing well. Others will be resistant as well."

I was shocked and hurt by this. I was still being used for purposes I didn't even know.

"How much longer will I be used without knowing what I'm being used for?"

"Now that you know the power within you. Never again."

"But won't I be forced to fight? Use my abilities for the sake of war?"

"Those are fights you have to choose for yourself. Decide if it's worth taking part. But that will always be up to you."

The women of Infinity already saw the morale benefits of my artwork. They hadn't ever pressured me about the chip and I didn't feel they ever would. Naomi could go off and do her experiments if she liked, but I didn't have to be a part of it. It was too late for me to take back anything she'd gotten off me. I had to trust and hope she used whatever she gained from me to do the right thing. If she didn't, I would have to find a way to remind myself there wasn't a reason to feel guilt over that.

However, there was guilt creeping in over something I would never be absolved of. Something I would never be able to take back.

"Can I ask you something?"

"Sure."

"Do you ever get over killing?"

"No."

"Never?"

"You don't. You just learn to carry it with you. To live with it. Despite its weight and hold on you. You have to carry on."

"I'm sorry I judged you so harshly on that. I didn't know better."

"You were still right. Taking a life is a dark matter."

I could feel his mind returning to a past memory. Someone completely shrouded in black stood before him with a gun. Indigo shot first. When he uncovered their face, a young woman's dead eyes stared back at him. She couldn't have been more than twenty.

There were other memories his brain returned to, but I didn't ask him about any of them. I wouldn't that night. He would tell me in time.

"Sometimes you have to take a life for other lives to be spared." Indigo said, after returning his mind to the here and now. To us.

"Such as yours?"

"Mine and yours."

Aziel said something similar in his twisted way. But it was the truth. There were times lives needed to end to protect others. If I left Aziel alive, he would have continued to kill again and again. He would have wanted me to as well. How many more deaths would I have been haunted by as time went on? That would have been true hell on earth, a fate worse than death. Perhaps my resistance would have turned him against me. Or my growing abilities would have made him feel it was safer to end me.

Knowing this didn't make it hurt any less.

The look in Indigo's eyes gave me a sense of knowing and acknowledgment of what I'd endured for him. What I'd continue to endure for the rest of my days in exchange for saving him. Being haunted by his death would have been the death of me as well. In the end, I would have done the same thing over and over again to save him.

"We'll carry that together now." I squeezed his hand.

"Yeah." He said.

Chapter Forty-Nine

Indigo was still asleep when I woke to the patter of raindrops on the roof. A nightmare about Aziel made me not quite ready to return to the realm of dreams for a little while. Until I got my bearings back. I couldn't even remember what happened in the dream, I just remembered seeing his face, eyes staring into my soul, communicating his hurt and betrayal.

The hollowness with Aziel being gone was sinking into me, making me feel a numbness to keep the pain away. There was a great sense of loss I didn't even feel when I left home for the last time. A part of me was dead now too. Not like a missing limb, friend, or comrade. This was something else, I'm not sure if anyone else could understand, except me and him. The part Aziel created. The part he created for me to be connected to him. Part of him forever. His selfishness was going to cost me for the rest of my life.

But it was a part which needed to die. Much of it still had.

My gaze returned to the man sharing my bed.

Indigo's roots ran even further into me. Deeper than Aziel's ever had, even if our connection was a unique one. Indigo reached to depths I didn't even know I had. Places I hadn't even known I contained. Scars and memories, I did my best to forget. Strengths I hadn't even known I had. Dreams I continued running towards when all else failed me.

There were certain connections even technology couldn't create or trace. There was nothing dark or suffocating about it. I didn't feel the need to escape from it all. Or run away. It gave me strength to face everything I needed to. Everything Aziel and the chip left behind. Everything I'll needed to face in its wake.

What had Indigo bore for me? More than I knew, perhaps more than I'd ever fully know even with the power left from the chip. More than I could ever show gratitude for. I wasn't there for many of those years he suffered because of me, but I could feel that he took on so much for the sake of my honor.

I kissed him and stroked his hair. Just to remind myself he was really there. Let it sink in to his unconscious mind I would always be there for him now. Do whatever I needed for him to repay him for everything he'd done for me.

***

Sunrise woke us both. We lounged in bed. I certainly wasn't going to train today. We let ourselves rest and no one came to disturb us from our glorious opportunity to be lazy.

"You know, I worked myself so hard to try to tell myself you could never save me. But those dreams you put in my head all those years ago, they kept me going. I was just so beat down as a kid. And I let myself stay down. But those dreams, kept me alive." I said to Indigo.

He smiled in turn.

"You literally saved my life twice. I think we're good. We can play on an even field now."

"I'm a Cyborg. That chip changed me so much."

"You're still you. That's never changed. Despite everywhere you've been. Everything you've been through. Everything you've survive. You never stopped being Sky."

"How about when I was Keira?"

"You were Sky even then. You proclaimed this to me even when we were young. You were always Sky. I was always your Indigo."

"You deserve a normal girl. Not a Cyborg."

"I'm certainly more than satisfied with what's in front of me."

I laughed a little.

"I haven't been the nicest to you Indigo. I don't think a loving relationship should start that way. Or get that way. You're better off starting new with a girl who can be good to you from day one."

"I love you and only you. I would like it if you stuck around."

"I've always loved you too, Indigo. I've just been afraid to admit it to you. But mostly, afraid to admit it to myself. Now I want to give you the world in return."

Indigo began to kiss me then. We ended up giving ourselves to each other for the second time. We got lost in each other's blue. But we were also finding other hues in each other, deeper complexities. The depths of the human experience we could understand. What of our existence which went beyond that which we couldn't. We swam and loved in it all.

***

I had fears about what the future would bring. But I didn't at the same time. Things seemed to continue to work out despite the tragedy and sense of doom others liked to blanket the world with. I had been guilty of that as well. Humanity hadn't destroyed the world with technology. The world hadn't destroyed technology. Technology hadn't killed humans off. People hadn't killed off the world or each other. There would always be those who would rise about the problems of the world and keep it going in a better direction. But there was more to it, something higher I could feel now more than ever. It couldn't just be luck. Not after this long. Not after the history humanity and this planet has had. Infinity was onto something with their beliefs.

I was a mother to a power I never asked for. I never consented to. And I didn't even know fully about until the effects were rooted so deeply into me, that they would remain part of me even after the chip was removed. Something that would be a part of me until I died.

I wasn't sure what I was going to use it for. Was I to be a tool of war? Of salvation? Or simply love. That was for me to decide.

At twenty I thought my life would soon be over. Now I was seeing it was just beginning. My life had so much more to it. There was so much I was going to have to do. So much more I was going to have to be. So much more I wanted to do. Even though I was now part of war, I don't feel like my whole life was such a fight anymore.

This was far from over. Others would be looking for me when they discovered what I could do. I couldn't predict all of the challenges I would be facing. Yet life now held a beauty and promise for me that I cherished with all my heart.

Nature found a way. As had technology. As had life and humanity. So would I. And so would Indigo and I with each other.

But there was one last thing I needed to wrap up.

Chapter Fifty

Indigo offered to go with me. I told him not to. He knew I was alive. He'd seen that. I needed to do this alone.

I returned to the Rainbow Valley cemetery the police department created for children lost to unsolved cases. My old backpack was full and heavy. But I was strong enough to carry this now.

As I slowly walked to my grave I wondered to myself, how many here were just like me? Not gone at all, but had simply found themselves elsewhere? Who were able to begin life anew? How many were never given that chance and just remained victims? Looking around, I realized I never would know. Intuition and technology could only go so far. I just hoped there were others out there like me, who were able to have another chance. Escape whatever shackled them and reached sweeter ground. Found life. Found themselves.

I wondered if anyone still mourned my grave. Felt bad for the girl who wasn't given much choice. I hoped they didn't. Keira never was really me.

I pulled out the hammer and stared at the message carved in blue rock before me.

Keira Aurora 2100-2114

May the life beyond this one fulfill your deepest wishes and most fantastic dreams.

I stood there with the hammer. Prepared to destroy Keira's mark forever. The upside-down hammer glared with sunlight at her name.

I lifted it in preparation of its destruction.

I hesitated. I couldn't stop staring at her name.

I couldn't do it.

I dropped the hammer to the ground. This wasn't my style.

I dove back into my backpack and pulled out my paint instead.

***

I stared at my handwork when I finished. No one came to stop me. And it wasn't even nighttime. My electro currents were keeping everyone away. Sending their focus and to-do list elsewhere whenever they drew close to the cemetery. No one would enter until I was long gone.

I smiled at my handy work.

I left it all behind. All of those paints. My backpack. All of that other life. I knew I was never coming back. I was leaving this concrete jungle behind me. This part of my past was behind me now.

I didn't even feel a hint of sadness. I was overjoyed. Exhilarated. Realizing I was fully alive. Finally, in control of my future. My destiny.

***

As I explored my old haunts for the last time, visiting each mural I'd created in the area, I heard through a radio frequency that after a long hiatus, a new piece of mine appeared over Keira Aurora's grave. The signal played out in my mind. This was my first time picking up such a frequency, my emotional state likely made me receptive to it.

For hours I listened in. People were wondering if we were one in the same. Or if the two of us been close in life. They wondered what the artist knew others didn't. Or if it was a grave randomly chosen to explain to others it would be the death of me and my art. I laughed. I laid everything out so clearly and yet people sought to find more mystery. Searching for something deeper than what was there. That happened with most unsolved cases.

Years later, when I was able to pick up radio frequencies from the other side of the world, police dug up the remains and discovered the reproduction gene in the skull, proving that it didn't come from a dead person. They even compared it to DNA left behind at the grave from the stuff I left. It was a match. They knew Keira Aurora hadn't died a tragic death. That's all that mattered to me.

This motivated police to check some more of the remains as well. Turned out many of them had the same reproduction gene as well. Faking your death had been a fad for a few decades when things had started to get rough in the cities.

Perhaps many missing people presumed dead weren't after all. It was now likely the population hadn't dropped as much as people thought. Stressed by technology, perhaps people wanted to start life again elsewhere. Away from governments and cities. Return to nature and find harmony with the new world through that. The epidemic wasn't as hard hitting as people thought.

Who else had been able to start over and have a good life? Just like me. Perhaps my story wasn't so unique after all. I could be happy about that.

But to my surprise, no one dared altered what I did to Keira Aurora's tombstone. It was left as a beacon of hope.

Even years later I heard rumors which came from those still discussing the mystery of that grave.

I left so much of myself behind. Left so much of myself right in the open, and yet I was still safe.

And despite the risks of my new life, I was safe there too.

***

After I returned to the Infinity camp, feasting on my fill of salmon and blueberries. Then I brought Indigo to the tree of life. He was in just about as much awe as I was when I'd seen it for the first time. He traced his fingers up and down the bark. Drew his eyes over the suspended branches. It could feel already he was formulating how he would recreate the magnificent tree on paper. I was already seeing how his interpretation of it would look on the wall of my workshop.

"Will you wait with me here until the stars come out?"

Indigo looked up through the leaves, "I'd like to see how it looks here through the twilight."

The moon rose from the sea in all her brilliance. The sparkle of stars more abundant than the diamonds on earth. I felt Artemis and her Doe were close by, wandering through the dark forest. Owls hooted in harmony with all the other songs of the night.

I led Indigo by hand to the nearby shore. We sat at the edge of the ocean, gazing into the two abysses before us. Feeling closer to the ones we both contained. Savored the silence as we contemplated it all. I allowed him the privacy of his thoughts beyond that point.

As my eyes met the sea, I realized there was no need to plot my whole future. Indigo and I could move day by day. I would decide what would be my new mission going forward. I would choose who I would be.

Finally, after our long silence, Indigo returned his gaze to mine.

"You ready?"

"Yeah," I said.

About Paige Etheridge

Of Athenian descent, Paige Etheridge is a Black Belt in Shaolin Kempo Karate, a Pisces Sun/ Leo Moon/ Aries Ascendant, a Taoist and a compulsive writer. A graduate of the SUNY Purchase's highly selective Lily Lieb Port Writing program for Creative Writing (where she carried a second major in History), Paige is an ex-MMA journalist who has been published in several magazines, including *Inked.*

Paige lives near Virginia Beach with her Police Officer husband Scott and her dog Athena. Paige and Athena walk every day despite the weather. She is an avid cook and gardener and tends to binge on True Crime, Gaming, Astrology and Paranormal YouTube videos. Paige loves old rock music and is a fan of Metal Gear Solid games, which she admits to playing constantly.

Cyber Knot is Paige's second novel.

Social Media

Instagram: https://www.instagram.com/paige.etheridge/

Facebook: https://www.facebook.com/paige.etheridge

LinkedIn: https://www.linkedin.com/in/paige-etheridge-21370b46

Twitter: https://twitter.com/PaigeEtheridge1

Goodreads:
https://www.goodreads.com/author/show/18754073.Paige_
Etheridge

Amazon: https://www.amazon.com/Paige-
Etheridge/e/B07MHJW92Q

Acknowledgments

To Max Rogers, thank you so much for the incredible advice and insight as I was working on this book. To Anthony Grilli, thank you for providing your expertise. To Arielle "R2Ninjaturtle" Sommerville, thank you for providing the amazing cover, aiding in my final decisions on story details, as well as your incredible support. To my husband Scott Schneider, for always providing enthusiastic backing and pride in all my projects. To Brett Kaplan, Ian Johnson, and Deidra Catero for the support. To my mother Terri Roughton and stepdad Ralph Roughton for amazing business advice. To the Solstice Family for aiding me as I start my career writing novels.

To Gaby Jacobson, thanks for giving Aziel his name. Thank you to all the fans who voted for the sake of my novels and the incredible support.

If you enjoyed this story, check out these other Solstice Publishing books by Paige Etheridge:

Kissing Stars Over the Rising Sun

Emerging from the ashes of Post WWII Japan, the Pan Pan were born. Transforming themselves into the antitheses of what Japanese women were supposed to be; they were the loud, vulgar, and independent lovers of the American GIs occupying their land. For many of these Women of the Night, it became more about pleasure and riches than survival; burning brightly for a few years before being wiped out by the Japanese themselves. Nearly erased from history for being too wild. This is the story of one of these women. Her name is Miyako.

https://www.amazon.com/Kissing-Stars-Over-Rising-Sun/dp/162526867X

CPSIA information can be obtained
at www.ICGtesting.com
Printed in the USA
BVHW040341270419
546721BV00017B/340/P